W9-BKN-953

DISCLAIMER:

This book about your disgusting head, called *Your Disgusting Head,* contains all the essential information you would ever need about your disgusting head. Accordingly, it covers, thoroughly, your mouth, your nose, and your ears. Because they are irrelevant and should be removed, this text will not make reference to the following:

Your ugly, boring brain

Your dumb hairline

Your hair — also dumb

Your dumb eyebrows

Your dorky "strongest-bone-in-your-body" jaw

Your lame skin which is so lame
I can't describe how lame it is

Your loser dimples

Your cheeks, which do not deserve to be mentioned, even though I just mentioned them, thus giving them the biggest thrill of their lives

Your eyelashes, which are actually sort of nice

If you have complaints about how we have assembled this book, and about its omissions, you can write a letter to me, Dr. Doris Haggis-On-Whey. This letter should be typed, double-spaced, and should be printed on heavy-bond paper, of an off-white variety. It should be no shorter than two pages, and should incorporate many semicolons, but no exclamation points. Do not use adverbs and please, *please,* avoid homonyms. When you have finished your letter complaining about this book, place it in an air-mail envelope, and attach to it the appropriate postage. Now walk to the post office, and once close to the post office, find the first garbage receptacle you can, and insert it into said receptacle, because frankly, I don't care what you think about the omissions in this book.

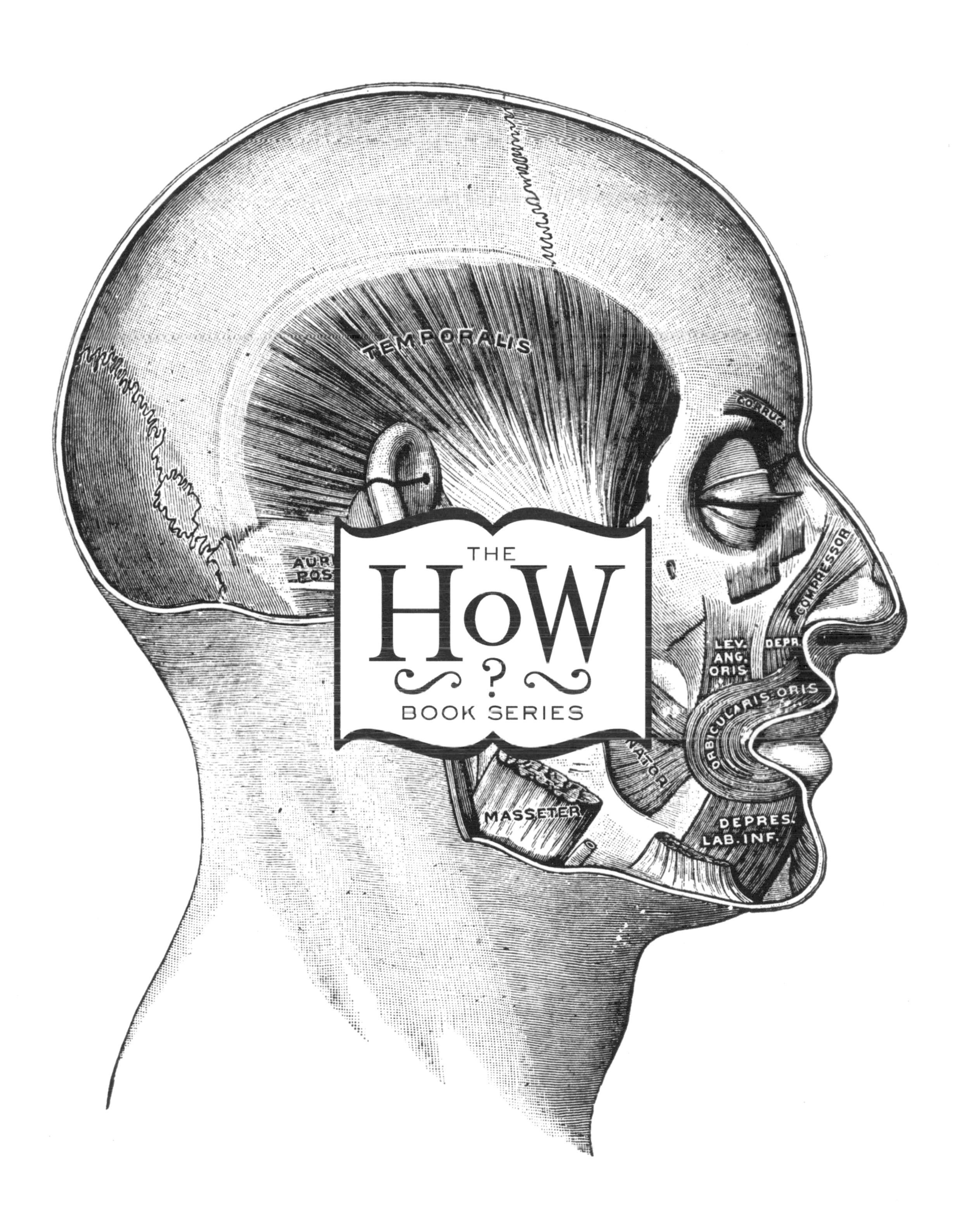
THE
HoW
?
BOOK SERIES
TEMPORALIS
CORRUG.
COMPRESSOR
LEV.
ANG.
ORIS
DEPR.
ORBICULARIS ORIS
MASSETER
DEPRES.
LAB. INF.

SIMON & SCHUSTER
Rockefeller Center
1230 Avenue of the Americas
New York, NY 10020

This book is a work of fiction. Names, characters, places, and incidents either are products of the author's imagination or are used fictiously. Any resemblance to actual events or locales or persons, living or dead, is entirely coincidental.

Designed by Mark Wasserman and Irene Ng of Plinko.

Manufactured in Singapore.

10 9 8 7 6 5 4 3 2 1

Library of Congress Cataloging-in-Publication Data is available.

Published by the HOW Series, Dedicated to the Exploration and Dissemination of Unbelievable Brilliance.
The HOW Series is a division of the Brutus Blue Publishing Force, which is a division of McSweeney's Publishing, which is located on Earth.

Photographs of Dr. and Mr. Haggis-On-Whey by Meiko Arquillos.
Cover illustration by Michael Kupperman.

This book is dedicated to Svetlana Abrosimova, Jordan Adams, Chantelle Anderson, Mery Andrade, Janeth Arcain, Leigh Aziz, Elena Baranova, Adia Barnes, Lucienne Berthieu, Tully Bevilaqua, Biba Bibrzycka, Sue Bird, Debbie Black, Octavia Blue, Ruthie Bolton, Sandy Brondello, Coretta Brown, Edwina Brown, Kiesha Brown, Rushia Brown, Marla Brumfield, Erin Buescher, Annie Burgess, Alisa Burras, Janell Burse, Jennifer Butler, Edna Campbell, Dominique Canty, Swin Cash, Iziane Castro Marques, Tamika Catchings, Kayte Christensen, Courtney Coleman, Cynthia Cooper, Sylvia Crawley, Edniesha Curry, Allison Curtin, Stacey Dales-Schuman, Helen Darling, Anna DeForge, Tai Dillard, Tamecka Dixon, Bethany Donaphin, Katie Douglas, Margo Dydek, Simone Edwards, Teresa Edwards, Shalonda Enis, Barbara Farris, Allison Feaster, Marie Ferdinand, Ukari Figgs, Isabelle Fijalkowski, Cheryl Ford, La'Keshia Frett, Linda Frohlich, Kelley Gibson, Jennifer Gillom, Adrienne Goodson, Shaunzinski Gortman, Yolanda Griffith, Lady Grooms, Gordana Grubin, Becky Hammon, Lisa Harrison, Kristi Harrower, Jessie Hicks, Chamique Holdsclaw, Kedra Holland-Corn, Dalma Ivanyi, Niele Ivey, Deanna Jackson, Gwen Jackson, Lauren Jackson, Tamicha Jackson, Pollyanna Johns Kimbrough, Adrienne Johnson, Chandra Johnson, LaTonya Johnson, Shannon Johnson, Tiffani Johnson, Vickie Johnson, Asjha Jones, Merlakia Jones, Jung Sun-Min, Sheila Lambert, Amanda Lassiter, Kara Lawson, Betty Lennox, Lisa Leslie, Takeisha Lewis, Tynesha Lewis, Helen Luz, Mwadi Mabika, Hamchetou Maiga, Sonja Mallory, LaTonya Massaline, Nikki McCray, Nicky McCrimmon, Danielle McCulley, Teana McKiver, Taj McWilliams-Franklin, Chasity Melvin, Coco Miller, Kelly Miller, Tausha Mills, DeLisha Milton-Jones, Tamara Moore, Astou Ndiaye-Diatta, Deanna Nolan, Vanessa Nygaard, Murriel Page, Wendy Palmer, Michaela Pavlickova, Ticha Penicheiro, Jocelyn Penn, Bridget Pettis, Tari Phillips, Plenette Pierson, Elaine Powell, Lynn Pride, LaQuanda Quick, Felicia Ragland, Semeka Randall, Kristen Rasmussen, Jamie Redd, Ruth Riley, Jennifer Rizzotti, Crystal Robinson, Nykesha Sales, Sheri Sam, Nakia Sanford, Kelly Schumacher, Georgia Schweitzer, Olympia Scott-Richardson, K.B.Sharp, Gergana Slavtcheva, Aiysha Smith, Katie Smith, Tangela Smith, Charlotte Smith-Taylor, Michelle Snow, Dawn Staley, Kate Starbird, Andrea Stinson, Tammy Sutton-Brown, Sheryl Swoopes, Penny Taylor, Nikki Teasley, LaToya Thomas, Stacey Thomas, Alicia Thompson, Tina Thompson, Erin Thorn, Slobodanka Tuvic, Mfon Udoka, Petra Ujhelyi, Michele Van Gorp, Kamila Vodichkova, Ayana Walker, DeMya Walker, Ann Wauters, Teresa Weatherspoon, DeTrina White, Stephanie White, Tamika Whitmore, Adrian Williams, Natalie Williams, Rita Williams, Shaquala Williams, Tamika Williams, Sophia Witherspoon, Brooke Wyckoff, and most especially Lindsey Yamasaki.

The authors would like to grudgingly acknowledge these earlier books, which had no real influence on this book, except in showing how not to write a reference book about the human head, which is disgusting:
Charles and Dixie Newcastle, *The Human Head Is So Very Nice: Let's Look Inside!*
Robert Burns and Lowell Hamilton, *The Mysteries of the Head Spread Out Before You like Cheese and Salad*
Barney Phillip, *Adventures in the Inner Ear Which Are Interesting for People like Me but Perhaps Not for Normal People*
Cynthia Rambeau, *I Like Noses! Here's Why and When*
Katherine Fuller, *The Mouths of Dogs, and Why They Are in Dogs and Not You, and Why This Distinction Is Crucial in a Democracy*

www.haggis-on-whey.com
www.mcsweeneys.net

ISBN 0-7432-6725-7

For information regarding special discounts for bulk purchases, please contact Simon & Schuster Special Sales at 1-800-456-6798 or business@simonandschuster.com

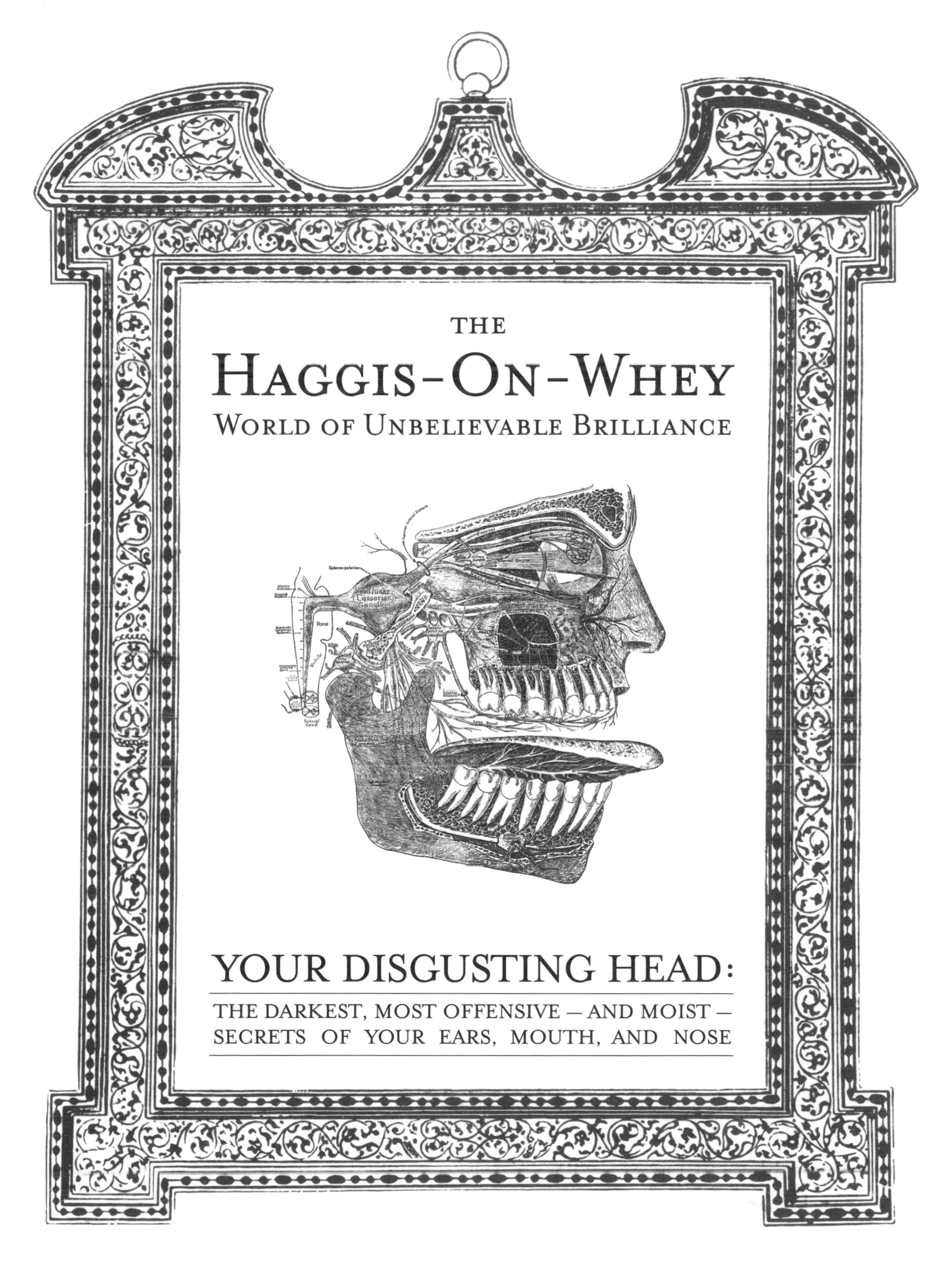

THE

HAGGIS-ON-WHEY

WORLD OF UNBELIEVABLE BRILLIANCE

YOUR DISGUSTING HEAD:

THE DARKEST, MOST OFFENSIVE — AND MOIST — SECRETS OF YOUR EARS, MOUTH, AND NOSE

SIMON & SCHUSTER
NEW YORK LONDON TORONTO SYDNEY

WELCOME! TO

Dr. and Mr. Doris Haggis-On-Whey's World of Unbelievable Brilliance

Greetings, Readers of this Brilliant Book. You have made a very smart decision in picking up this book. Indeed, you have made a life-changing choice. Your very life has already been changed!

Do you feel different already? Do you feel taller, or heavier, or less likely to fall into wells? These are all common side effects of reading my books, the books written and authored by me, me being Dr. Doris Haggis-On-Whey, your hero and best friend, also known as the Most Extraordinary of Reclusive Scientists Who Know All and Reveal as Much as the Lesser-Minded Can Understand. Other side effects of reading this masterwork include drowsiness and dizziness and mild paranoia. Do not eat food whilst reading this book! Also: do not use the word *whilst.*

As I stated in my first book, *Giraffes? Giraffes!*, I know everything that you don't, I tower over all scientists of all time, and am now in the process of sharing my findings, gathered over the course of many decades, with all of the fine-smelling people of the world, and also with people like you. I do this in hopes that you will use this knowledge — which includes the revelation that giraffes came not from some wack idea about "evolution," but from space, on very long conveyors, and now live in Indiana — for good, and not for evil, even the banal kind.

Joining me in this hope is my husband Benny, who for all these years has stood by me, and sometimes has crouched behind me, hoping I would fall. This kind of thing makes him laugh. Benny enjoys almonds, too, and socks when they are warm. I love Benny, and accept him for what he is. There is a good deal more information about myself and Benny on page fifty-eight. That is not an invitation to read this book out of order. That would be wrong.

In case you are wondering, there will be no information at all in this book about your nose in the Old West. I realize that most books which cover your disgusting head include entire chapters called "Your Nose in the Old West," or "The Old West and Your Nose," or "The Old West, Gold, Your Nose, and Smelting." Well, this is one book that will contain none of those things. None! I have proven again and again that your nose played no part whatsoever in the Old West, a time that I seriously doubt ever happened.

That is all,

Doris Haggis-On-Whey PhD, MS, DDS   BENNY

Dr. and Mr. Doris Haggis-On-Whey

WHERE YOUR MOUTH HAS BEEN

The first thing we need to cover is the obvious: where has your mouth been? Oftentimes we, as citizens, come home from work or trips or pilates and we are asked, by whoever occupies our homes with us, Where has your mouth been? Sometimes there are objects, like food and cement, inside of our mouths, or attached to the side. Other times we have a crazed look on our faces, and smell of shrubbery. In either case, we need to answer the question.

This locale, approximately thirty miles from the northern tip of Finland, is about as fake-looking as a real-life place can look. Do you know they have a hotel made entirely out of ice? Ice chairs, ice beds, mints made from ice put on your ice-pillow — this place has everything! In Lapland, for the price of four U.S. dollars your mouth had two teams of sleigh dogs, a three-bedroom igloo, and its own congressional seat.

One day your mouth got kicked out of this guy named Maurice's VW van and found out two hours later that he was in Portland, Oregon, or Washington, or wherever it is. The people of Portland all walk very slowly, because gravity works differently there.

Did you know that in 1952 the Faeroe Islands harvested 87,961 tons of cod? Sure did. That's when the king of Denmark, whose name is Steve, gave the Islands the extra "e" they now use so proudly. Until 1952, the place was called the Faroe Islands, which is not nearly as cool as the Faeroe Islands, which became its name because of all that cod.

Your mouth doesn't even want to talk about its trip to Uruguay. "Actually, you know what," it just told me, "it's about time I told someone." When your mouth went to Uruguay, things went badly from the beginning, when its luggage was stolen by a team of toddlers working in tandem. Wait, did I say Uruguay? I meant Paraguay. Your mouth has never been to Uruguay. My bad.

Your mouth had a layover between Mongolia and the Canary Islands and the Holiday Inn in Budapest always has the best pools, so that explains that. However, it does not explain how your mouth — that same night! — suddenly became the traveling manager for the Stockholm Stingers, the top basketball team in Sweden. Not to mention how our mouth found itself banned from both the hotel's men's exercise room and also its gift shop. Man, your mouth has been around.

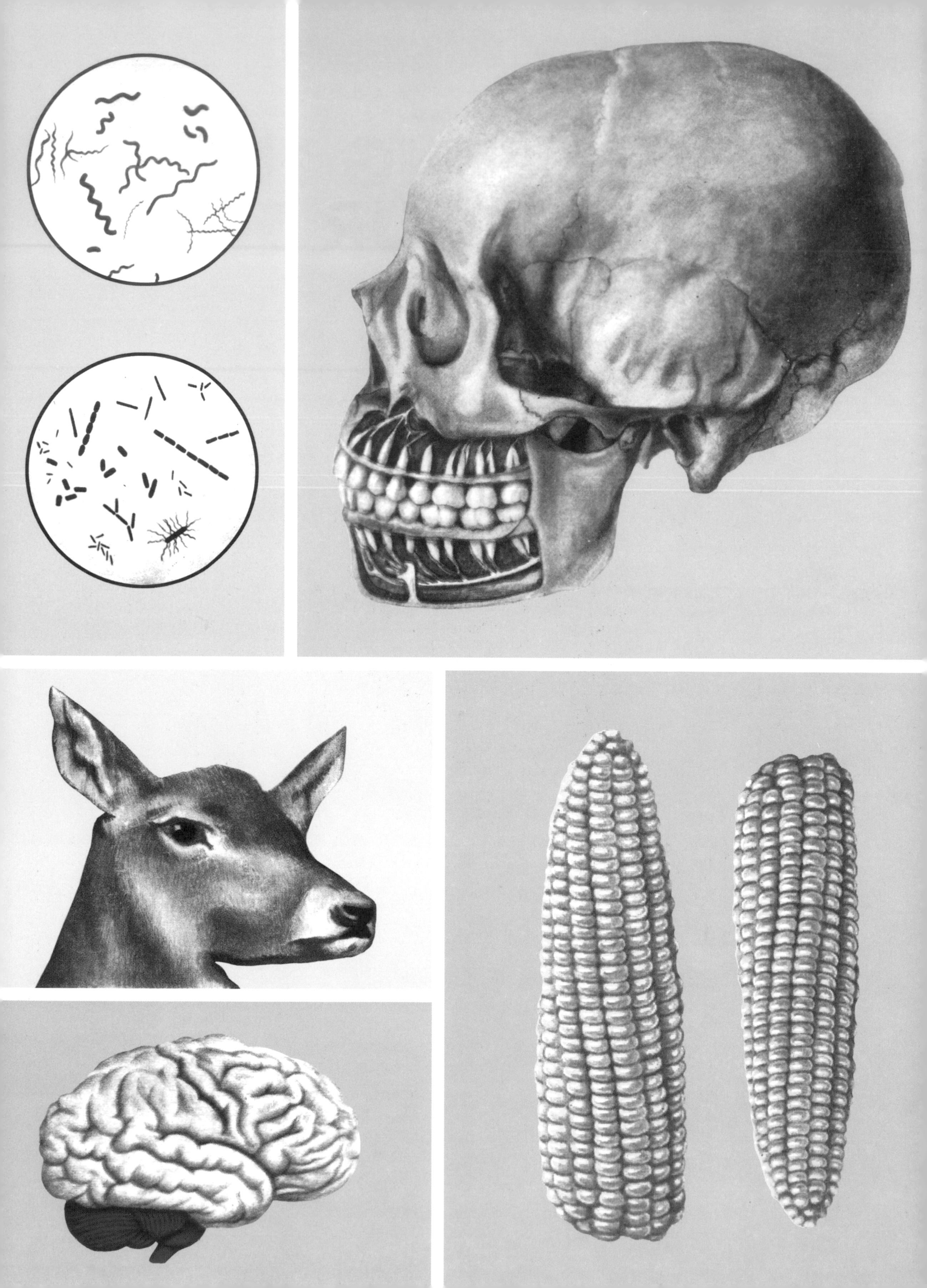

THE JUICES, OILS, GOOS, GUNKS, OOZES, AND SAPS THAT MAKE UP YOUR HEAD ARE OF MANY TYPES, AND OCCUPY MANY DIFFERENT PLACES IN YOUR HEAD. HERE IS A GUIDE, NOW AND FOR ALWAYS, TO:

THE SICKENING FLUIDS THAT FILL YOUR SKULL

There are over 1,100 known fluids in your skull and face, and they are all uniformly repulsive and most of them smell like soap when it has been dropped in tar. For centuries, scientists have attempted to categorize these fluids, to no avail. Most recently, a team from Holland tried, but these Hollandnese scientists were too tall to fit into their labs, and gave up. What makes it so hard to catalog all of these liquids and jellies? First of all, they are very slippery. Secondly, some of them are invisible to the naked eye. Thirdly, have you ever had a headache caused by a husband who is trying to learn to play the cello but thinks he can do so without a bow? Have you had a husband, named Benny, who just sort of bangs on the cello like it's a drum or kitten? It can be very distracting when you're trying to make sense of the putrid crud that fills our heads.

FLUID	NICKNAME	LOCATION	FUNCTION
Snot	"Snotty"	Nose, back of throat	None
Saliva	"Spitty"	Mouth	None
Drool	"Drooly"	Mouth, couch, bed	Public humiliation
Blood	"Red"	Brain, nose, ears	None
Boogers	"Boogeyman"	Nose, fingers	For hobbyists
Wax	"Lefty"	Ears	Smells interesting
Pus	"Pus-Man"	Nose, ears, brain	None
Goop	"MC G-Star"	Back of throat	Makes voice sound froggy
Spittle	"Spittle-izzle"	Corner of mouth	Impresses the ladies
Ooze	"Ms. Oozey"	Brain	None known
Gunk	"Dr. Gunkmeister"	Brain	Helps with memories of accidents with food
Plasma	"J. Plasma Funkmasta"	Brain, neck, face (under)	Tells jokes, some are funny
Sap	"Johnny Sap"	Upper nose, lower ear	None

WHO IS THE LUNATIC WHO DESIGNED YOUR EARS?

They are ugly things, ears. Look at your hands. See how clean they are, how simple the lines are, how efficient the design is? Your feet are slightly less good-looking, yes, but your ears are just wrong.

The ear was invented and designed by Fernando de la Mancini-Goldfarb, in 1911, which was also a good year for yeast. One day in March, de la Mancini-Goldfarb was assigned by the kings of Spain, France, Montenegro, and Atlanta to design a part of the body that would help humans hear sound and hold wax. De la Mancini-Goldfarb, who had until then only designed a few shoes and animals (including the dreaded Komodo Dragon and the less-dreaded nearsighted river otter), took the job with great enthusiasm.

The problem was, he only had two days to do it, and he was already busy with building a tree fort for his three sons, Piero, Giacomo, and Bucky. They really wanted the tree fort built right away, because their father Fernando did not smell good and thus their house did not smell good, and thus they were hoping to sleep outside as much as possible. So de la Mancini-Goldfarb did not have as much time to design the ears as he'd have liked, and finally spent one long sleepless night trying to get it right. Unfortunately, as the night went on, de la Mancini-Goldfarb's ear designs went from respectable to plain stupid.

Designing an ear wouldn't be so hard, would it? One would only need to design a sound-capturing device, which would "cup" the sound from the air and bring it into the brain. It seems like an easy assignment, even for someone doing it quickly, and wearing goofy little boots.

But as the night wore on, de la Mancini-Goldfarb made what should have been a simple design more and more complicated, second-guessing his own better instincts and forever dooming us with terrible-looking things attached to our heads. Thank god for sideburns and earphones. And scissors.

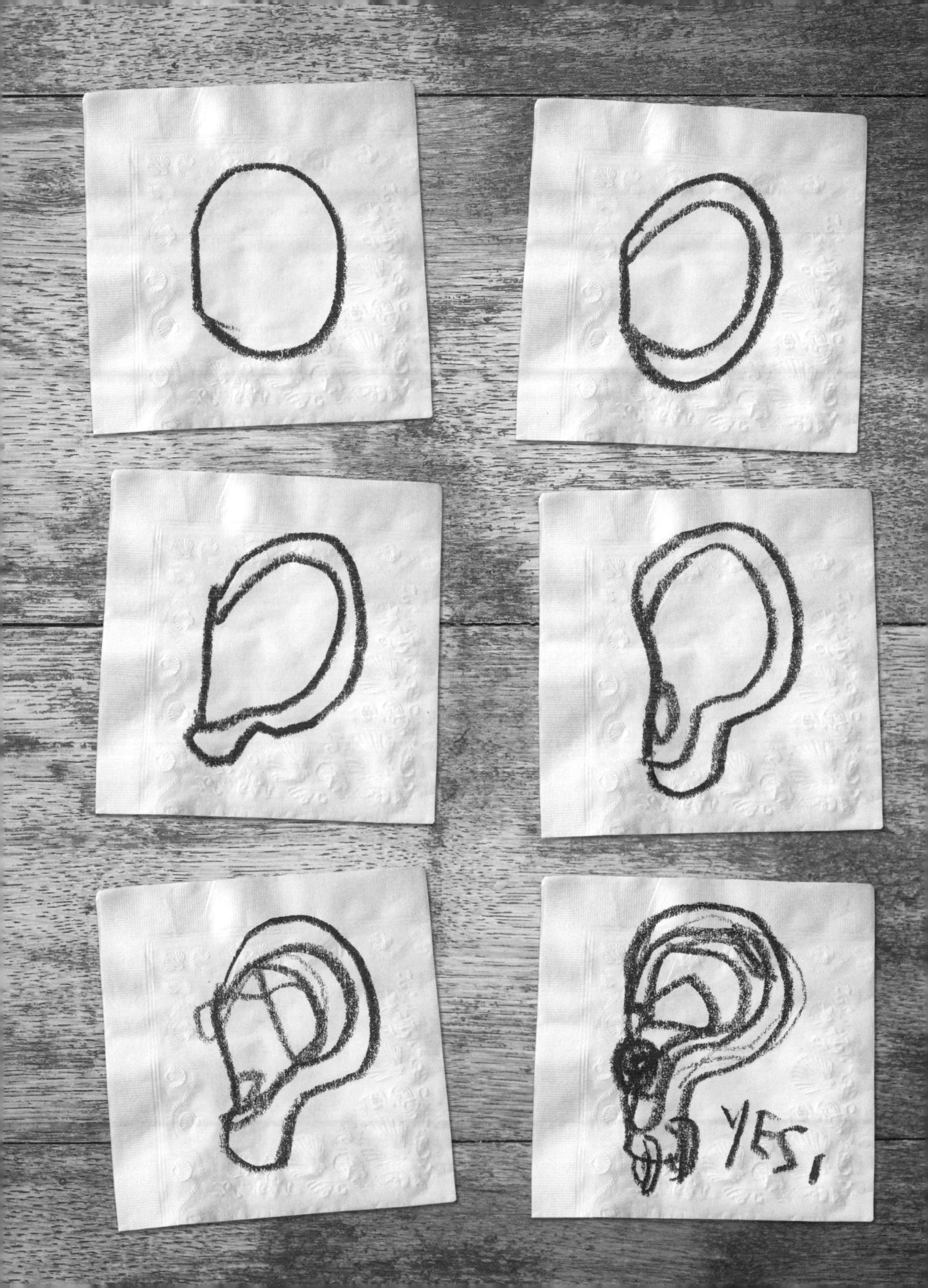
YES,

WHY YOUR BREATH SMELLS BAD

Your breath smells bad because you've been eating food that smells bad. But what makes the food smell bad? Aha! This is where you need my help. When you put your nose to certain foods, they might not initially smell bad — and in some cases they might even smell good. You might pick up an apple, which has a fresh scent, much like racoons and ballpoint pens. But what causes the apple, once in your mouth, to smell so not-good?

The fact is that the bad smell comes from you. Every time you put food in your mouth and start chewing it, you get that food all excited, and a chemical reaction takes over in that food, which causes it to make a bad smell. In short, your chewing makes the food sweaty. Like, armpit sweaty. You see, eating food is the most natural and common way in the world to make foods secrete their personal body odor, or PBO. Now, food PBO is sometimes rather obvious — cheese that smells bad smells worse when sweaty — but there are some food-PBOs that smell different than would be expected. Did you know a raisin's PBO smells like the teacher's lounge?

Look at the chart below, and see if you can connect the everyday food to the smell provoked when that food is chewed.

FOODS	PBO
1. Spinach	a. Herring
2. Sunflower seeds	b. Oranges
3. Raw meat	c. Baby powder
4. Kumquat	d. Dogs*
5. Bananas	e. Your parents' pillows
6. Ice-cream sandwich	f. Tennis balls
7. Cactus juice	g. Sweaty bananas

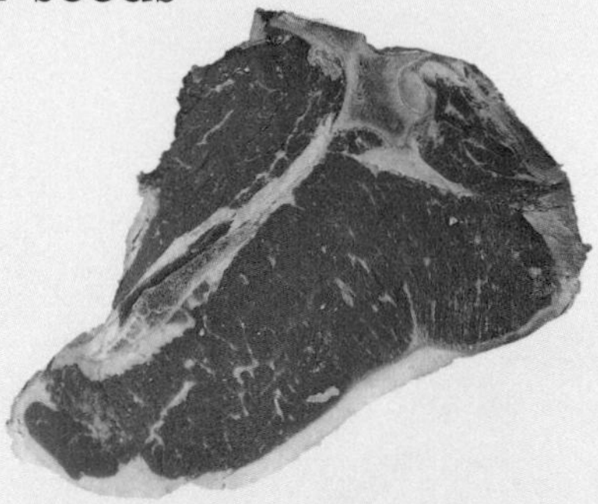

*Did I say dogs? I meant toast.

Correct answers: 1-d, 2-c, 3-b, 4-f, 5-g, 6-a, 7-e

REASONS TO REMOVE YOUR TEETH OR TONGUE

These things are removed for all sorts of reasons. Sometimes they are old and do not work properly. Sometimes they have started to smell bad or that item has ceased to look attractive to one's eye. Sometimes that thing had trouble balancing a state budget. All kinds of reasons! Just yank the thing!

REASONS FOR TEETH REMOVAL	REASONS FOR TONGUE REMOVAL
Dentist did it	Superintendent did it
Found better teeth, like on the ground	Found out it was put in backwards
Peer pressure	Peer pressure
Not sharp enough	Too sharp
Accident	"Accident"
Was blocking another tooth	MUTINY!
Suspected of enjoying flossing	Suspected of liking cabbage
Decay	TREASON!
Mouth politics	Mouth politics

EARWAX AND THE REAL STORY OF K.I.T.T.Y.

Have you ever gotten water stuck in your ear and then been forced to jump up and down to get rid of it? You get out of the shower or the dunk tank and suddenly you've got some ridonculous buildup of wax in just one ear and you just say to yourself, "Arrrrerreegghhghgh!"

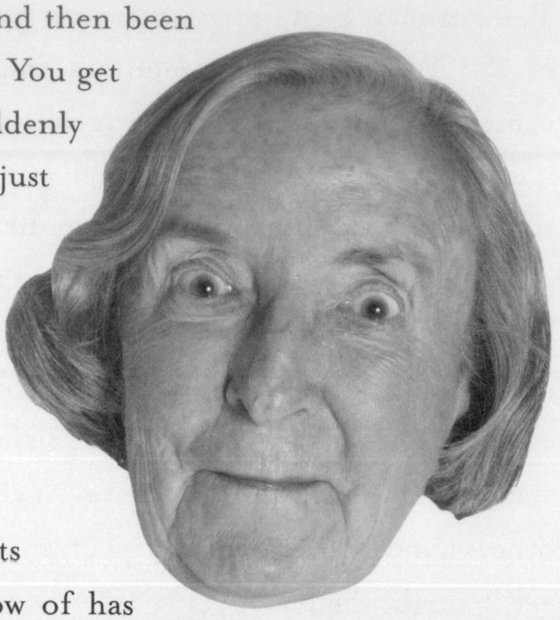

You are not alone. Such a phenomenon has even happened to yours truly. But I have no idea what causes it. Absolutely none. I want to blame it on the Danish, but won't.

However, as a doctor, I do know about earwax and its different colors. Every animal and plant you know of has a different color of ear gunk. People have a yellow- or greenish-brown-colored wax. Mammals have orangish-whitish-purple-colored wax. Houseplants have earwax of a bright red hue. But barracudas have none. No earwax at all. It's true. One day they voted on it and now they don't have any.

I believe it was 1980. That day it was warm and fair. The barracudas woke up to find they didn't actually have ears. They took a real close look and found that what they had always feared was a cold, hard truth. Their ears that they thought to be simply rather petite were simply absent. However, they still had earwax. A whole lot of it stuck to where their ears would be. Globs of it. And so they tried to change that and went to those who had the power to do so.

SHAPES OF BRAINS, INCLUDING THE POSSUM, AND COLORS OF EARWAX

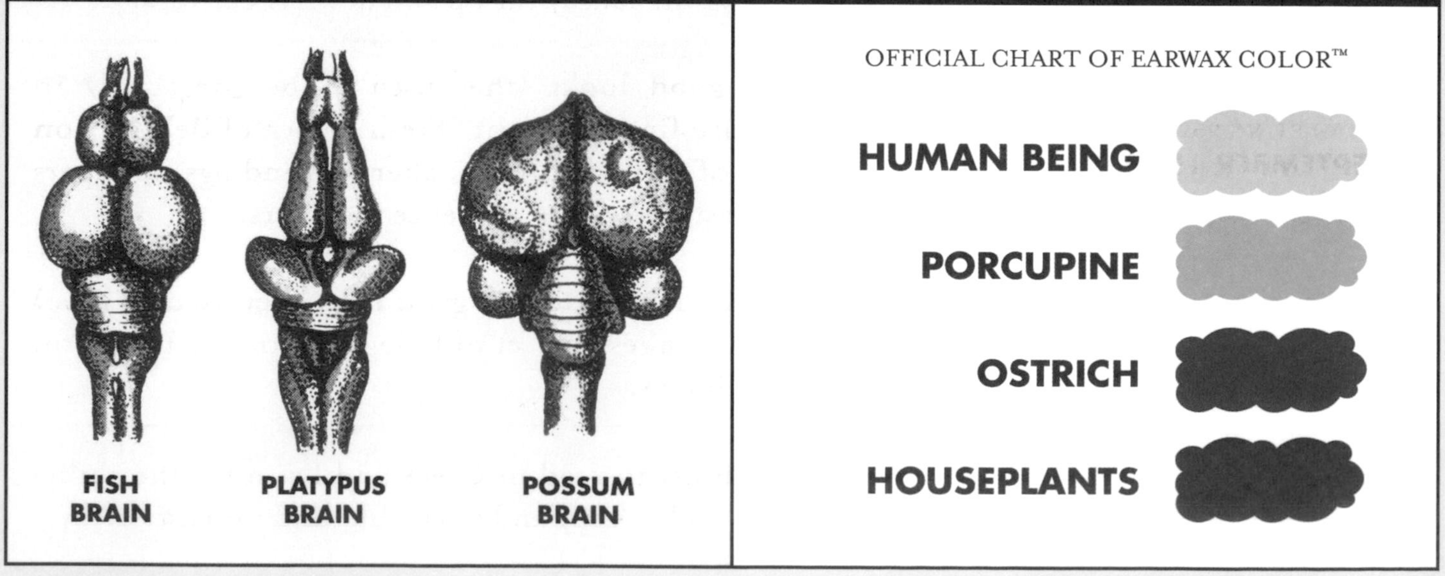

FISH BRAIN

PLATYPUS BRAIN

POSSUM BRAIN

OFFICIAL CHART OF EARWAX COLOR™

HUMAN BEING

PORCUPINE

OSTRICH

HOUSEPLANTS

The Animal Trait Re-Assigning Voting Commission, or K.I.T.T.Y., as it's sometimes known, has given us some amazing animal makeovers over the years. The way it works is as follows: every year, all animals gather over a simple potluck dinner, in Daytona Beach. There, a few select species can vote on which trait they currently own but would like to subtract, on what grounds, and what they would like to replace it with. In the barracudas' case, earwax was substituted for a scarf of fine cashmere. While many animals choose never to change themselves, others choose to take advantage of this every chance they get. Cough, the platypus.

SIR JOHN JOHN VON FERDINAND, THE FIRST PRESIDENT OF K.I.T.T.Y.

Still a bit confused on the concept? Here are a couple of other examples:

MEETING 172: **NOVEMBER 1918**	Penguins give up flight for a bigger tail.
MEETING 226: **AUGUST 1972**	Lions give up exuberance for a phat hairdo.
MEETING 238 (WIDELY KNOWN AS THE MOST CONTROVERSIAL): **MAY 1985**	Possums give up the power of speech in exchange for three autographed photos of Matthew Broderick.
MEETING 240: **OCTOBER 1987**	Monitor lizards give up wings for the ability to guess people's ages.
MEETING 244: **JULY 1991**	Rhinos give up the ability to perform complex mathematical equations for the chance to drive the family car up and down the driveway.
MEETING 252: **SEPTEMBER 1999**	Bats give up their good looks (they used to be gorgeous!) in exchange for the entire first season of "Fresh Prince of Bel-Air" on DVD, with all kinds of extras, outtakes, alternate endings, bloopers and interviews with cast, crew, and audience members.
MEETING 254: **JUNE 2001**	Bald eagles give up their hair (lots of great hair, they used to have) in exchange for a really awesome set of hologram stickers to put on their folders and textbooks.
MEETING 257: **AUGUST 2004**	Ferrets give up the ability to read in Greek and Latin for the ability to sneak around and look creepy and snake-like and untrustworthy.

THE FOUR GREATEST ORAL SURGERIES IN HISTORY (IN REVERSE ORDER)

Nº4 In 1927, Dr. Edward MacDemmy of Edinburgh, Alabama, was called in one day to treat a strange case. A patient one night had grown a set of shark's teeth just inside of his own teeth. The doctor began with one question: "What possessed you to start growing shark's teeth?" The patient could offer no explanation. Dr. MacDemmy continued, "I mean, what possible use could you have for them? Do you realize how hard those are to clean?" After some time alone, the doctor informed the patient that this nonsensical growth would have to be removed and that pain was to be expected.

SHARK TEETH ARE, LIKE, TOTALLY SHARP

DR. MACDEMMY, SHOWN HERE IN HAPPIER TIMES

That Sunday, Dr. MacDemmy attended the annual hospital bobcat race, at which he approached a group of his colleagues with his predicament with this patient who insisted on growing shark's teeth inside his regular teeth. The reaction from the other doctors could only be described as being one long, loud guffaw. It was at that moment that Dr. MacDemmy informed his colleagues of his solution to the problem, a procedure that was to utterly change the shape of modern medicine.

Dr. MacDemmy proposed applying "the tablecloth trick," widely known by magicians and lumberjacks, as a new experimental form of dental surgery. You know this trick: a clever person

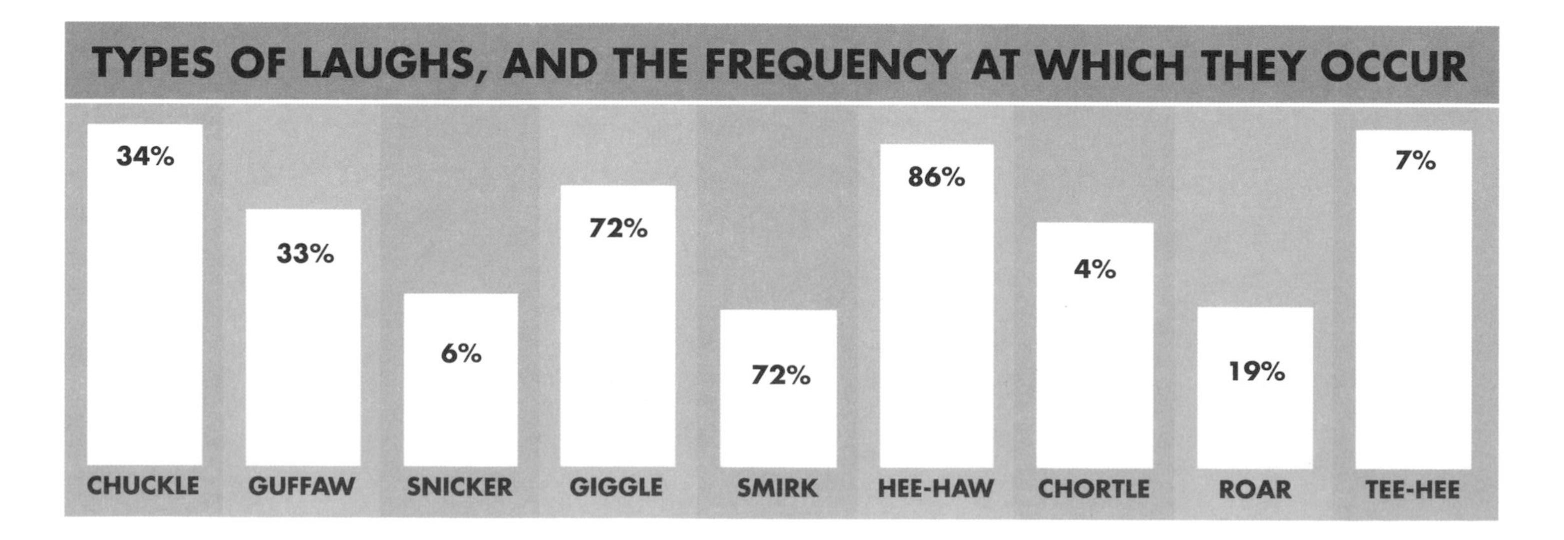

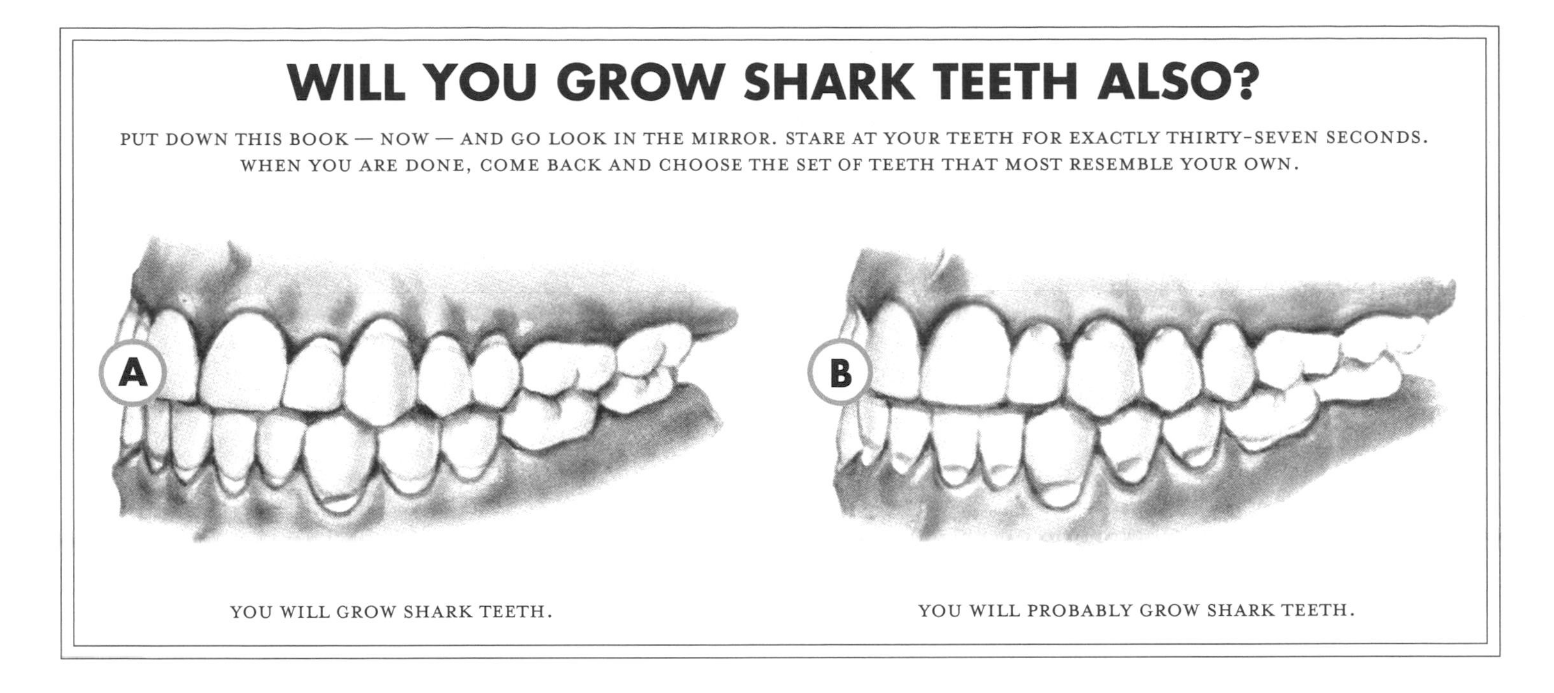

WILL YOU GROW SHARK TEETH ALSO?

PUT DOWN THIS BOOK — NOW — AND GO LOOK IN THE MIRROR. STARE AT YOUR TEETH FOR EXACTLY THIRTY-SEVEN SECONDS. WHEN YOU ARE DONE, COME BACK AND CHOOSE THE SET OF TEETH THAT MOST RESEMBLE YOUR OWN.

YOU WILL GROW SHARK TEETH.

YOU WILL PROBABLY GROW SHARK TEETH.

grabs a tablecloth and deftly yanks it out from under glasses and plates and the like, without disturbing said glasses and plates. In this way, Dr. MacDemmy was suggesting that he could somehow harness the shark's teeth and with a quick pull tear the teeth out, with the patient's mouth never the wiser. And yet even as Dr. MacDemmy was applying the tablecloth to the patient's mouth, the doctors were laughing. Then they laughed some more. And kept laughing for an uncomfortably long time. Then there was a break in the action when someone dropped some change on the floor and — cheapskate — he really wanted it back. When Dr. MacDemmy resumed, the doctors laughed once again and one even said, "Right, pfff." However, when Dr. MacDemmy made the cover of *Dentist Happenings* the next month none of those doctors were laughing. No, sir.

It appears that we're out of room, and have no space for Nos. 3-1. Which is too bad, because those ones, man they were sweet.

BEHOLD THE GREAT PHIL — THE MAGICIAN WHO INVENTED THE CLASSIC TABLECLOTH TRICK

THE ROOF OF YOUR MOUTH *THROUGH HISTORY!*

5800 B.C. The roof of your mouth changes from its prehistoric periwinkle color to the great pink-brown-red hue that we recognize today and has been imitated by so many designers.

2400 B.C. Begins the first entry in the longest continuous journal ever written by a part of someone's mouth.

997 B.C. Increased yawning makes it very dry.

266 B.C. Licked by tongue for 24,760,109th time.

104 B.C. Dressed in vinaigrette, nutmeg, and parsley and then is taken to the grand ball at Empress Claudiva's new summer house in Geneva.

503 B.C. Held underwater for four minutes, survives, seeks revenge — and gets it!

788 A.D. The roof of your mouth somehow gets involved in the great Battle for the Black Sea, between the Ottomans and a group called Jerry's Gang. Intense!

1121 A.D. Looks very pretty today but no one gives it one compliment. Not even one.

1345 A.D. Mistaken for a truffle and is eaten.

1690 A.D. Swollen, infected, and feeling bloated. Doctors say it might be a side effect of bronchitis. Others claim stage fright.

1966 A.D. Is nearly replaced by steel/aluminum alloy but the procedure is stopped at the last moment in a location mix-up.

1981 A.D. Stars in a popular sitcom called *That's the Roof of My Mouth!*, airing just after *Chico and the Man.* Due to the popularity of the show, is given its own variety show, *The Roof of Your Mouth and Dawn*, costarring one of Tony Orlando's former back-up singers. The show is very popular in the southeast and in Germany, but is cancelled after six episodes due to an outbreak of shingles on the set. Seriously, this amazing show was brought down by shingles. What kind of world allows such things?

2002 A.D. The roof of your mouth is short-listed for the Nobel Prize, but loses to some guy from Norway or Sweden or something. Favoritism? I can't get into it. Makes me too upset.

2003 A.D. The roof of your mouth wants the best for you.

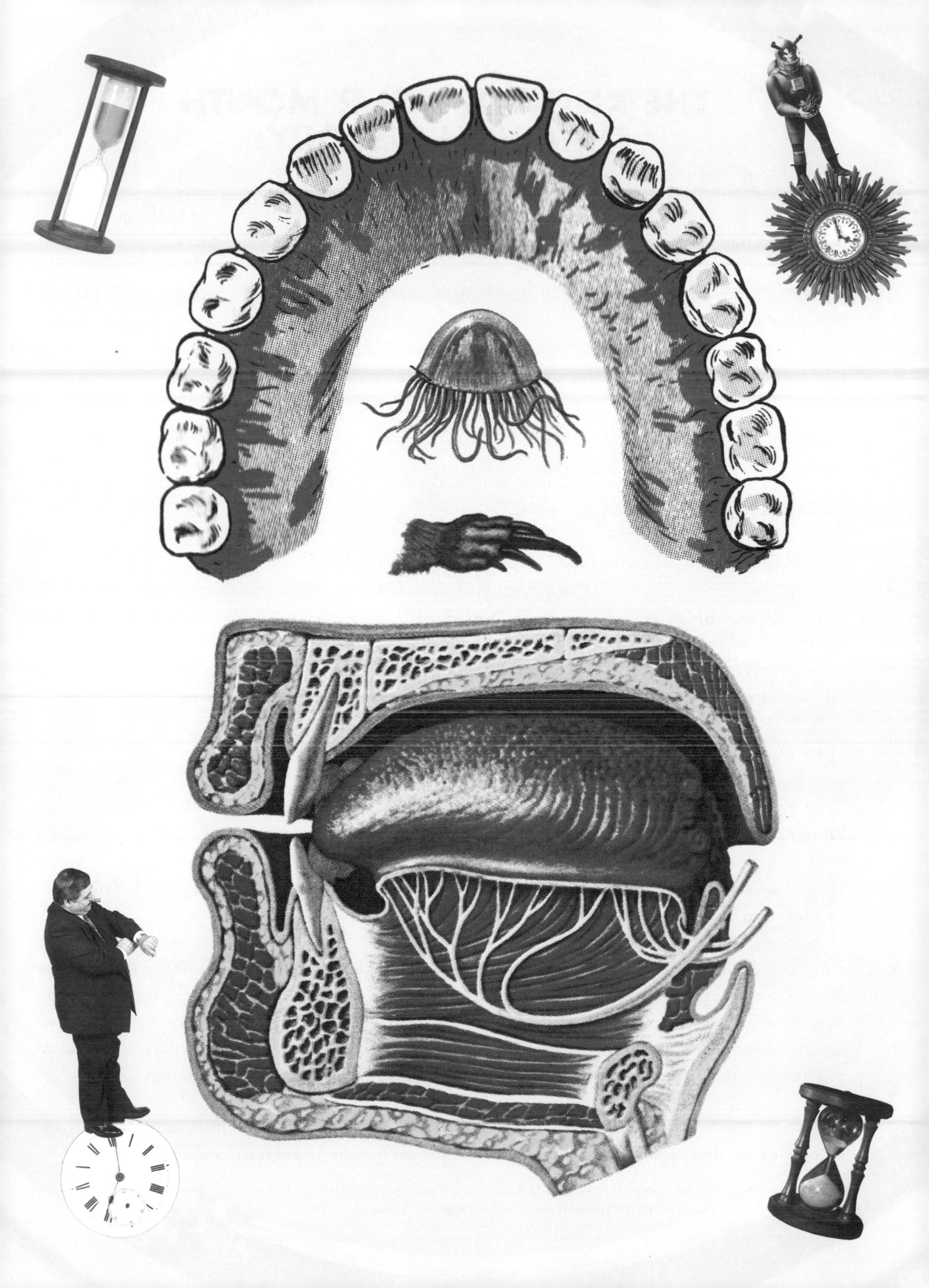

WHERE DOES ALL THE SNOT COME FROM?

Many average people, over the years, have sent me questions about science and nature and space and food. They do this because I know everything and am fearsome. They ask so many questions, from "Why do so many people think they know how to moonwalk?" to "Why are my new curtains on fire?" And always I have answers (Tangier; 1066). But the one question I am asked most often, 14,625 times so far, is this: where does all the snot come from?

Usually this question comes from citizens who are in the midst of a cold, or the flu. They find that they can blow their nose upwards of 100 times a day, and every single time, they fill their tissue with nasal output. How is that possible, they ask? Sometimes they weigh the snot for me (the most snot produced in one day: Paul Scola, Burlingame, CA: 11 pounds, 4 ounces), and one time, the questioner even sent me her collected snot, which she had secured in a mayonnaise jar. Note: In the future, if you are sending me your snot, please use a nonbreakable vessel.

It seems impossible that someone could produce and expel upwards of 12 pounds of snot in one day and not be dead. So the question is, where does all the snot come from?

And the answer is Detroit. It's the only place that could manufacture that much snot. As the world's largest producer of industrial snot, it only makes sense that they would also be supplying most of the world's personal use snot. There is your answer.

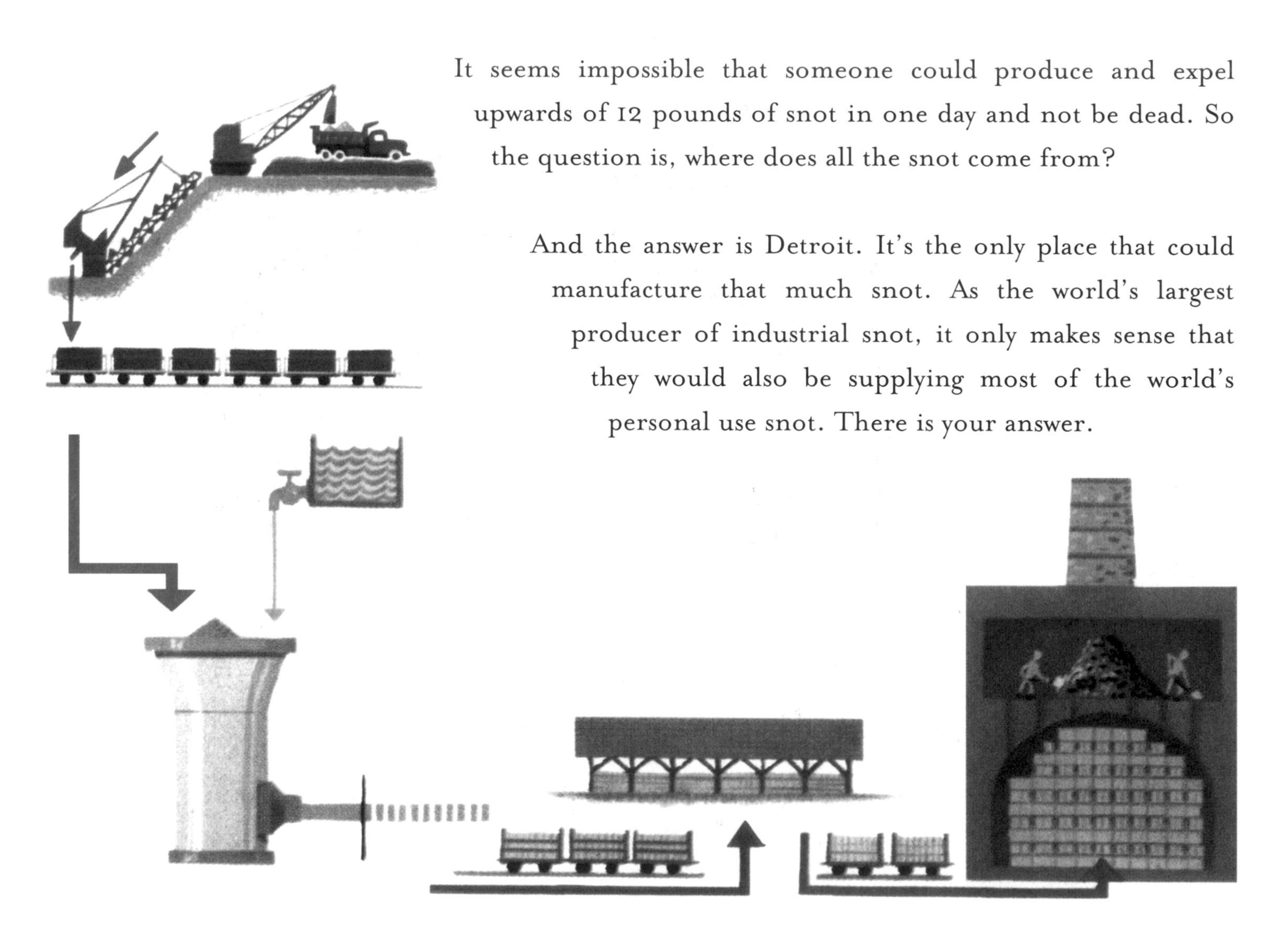

A PAINFULLY OBVIOUS DIAGRAM SHOWING THE HARVESTING AND PRODUCTION OF SNOT

PAUL SCOLA, CURRENT SNOT CHAMPION

HOW TO BECOME BETTER FRIENDS WITH YOUR GUMS

1. Try quizzing them about stuff

Your gums are very bright, even if their area of expertise is kind of small. Find out what they do know about and then ask them questions they'll know the answers to. Even better: if you have younger sisters or brothers, find them and bring them over. Now quiz both of them about the same questions. Look how happy your gums look, knowing they've beaten somebody! They love winning. They're in ecstasy.

2. Talk to them about the food they're about to receive

If you're sitting at home eating mashed potatoes with gravy, just say, "Soggy tators on the way! Heads up!" Or if you're eating noodles, tell your gums, "Hot strings on your porch! Watch it!" Or a nice chicken soft taco might prompt you to say, "Here it comes, amigos!" Your gums play no part in chewing or digestion but you should still tell them these things. Why? Because they're curious and that should be encouraged.

3. Ask them how they're feeling

Talking to someone about how they are now is a good way of getting to know how that person is all the time. It's true. It's a medical fact! However, this tactic can be a little dicey. If your gums start talking about bleeding a lot lately or smelling bad, quickly move down to step four.

4. Let people see them now and then

Sure, they're not very pretty. Heck, they're probably even downright ugly. Bumpy, discolored, strange, and often covered in small white globules that can be popped if you position your teeth just right. That's why our lips kindly hide your gums from the view of other people. Otherwise no one would ever talk to anyone else. It just wouldn't be worth it. But every so often, perhaps once a month or every few years, you should go into a room (candlelit!) with a friend or relative, and smile, using your fingers to pull your lips up. Your gums will feel like Cinderella!

5. Tell them they should get involved in politics

The one thing gums are most upset about is that they aren't allowed to vote. Like women did all over the world in the 20th century, your gums often hold protests, insisting that they be allowed to vote in national elections. And though I, Dr. Doris H-O-W, don't think your gums should vote on anything, ever — because they're loonies — you should listen to their whining and nod agreeably.

6. Remember to always be yourself

Your gums can tell a phony a mile away. Just play it straight and you'll be fine.

POLITICAL AFFILIATIONS WITHIN THE BODY

DEMOCRATIC PARTY

GUMS
↓
SHOULDER
↓
PUPILS
↓
TONSILS
↓
BLEEDING HEART
↓
ANKLE
↓
LEFT THUMB

REPUBLICAN PARTY

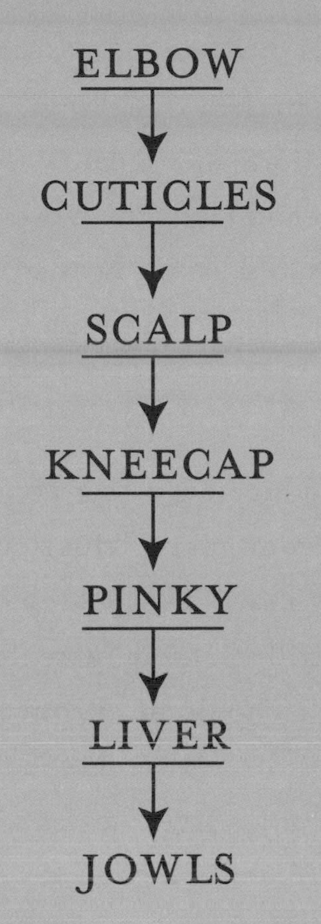

LIBERTARIAN PARTY

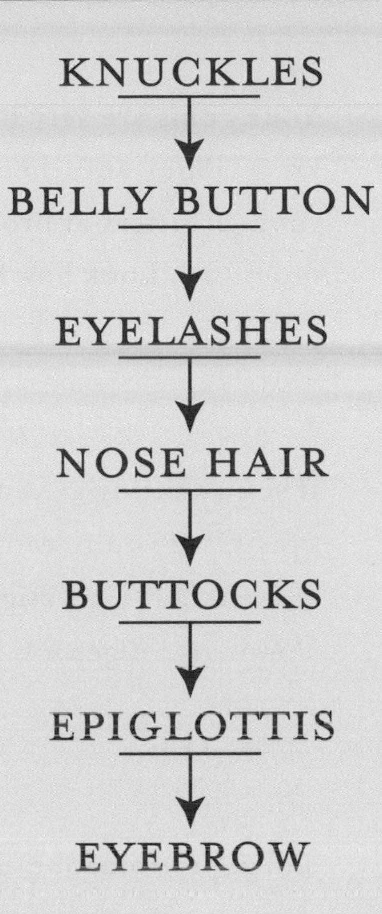

THE STORY OF THE MOST FAMOUS MOUTH IN THE WORLD

Now, to give you an idea of how famous this mouth is, let me just say that I can hardly remember the name of the owner of this mouth — it's Owen something, or something Owen. However, not a day goes by that the mouth's name — Professor Betsy Ann-Margaret Betsyson — does not pop most unexpectedly into my head. The defining trait of this mouth, Betsy, is not its complexity, but rather how very simple it is. Inside this mouth you shall not find the hundred stories of adventure and peril played out upon a set of hundreds of different teeth of all shapes and sizes. Instead, in this mouth you shall find only the number two, the total number of teeth in Betsy.

While the average person — you for instance, or someone normal — has these jagged, misshapen teeth that fight, bite, and claw for space in your mouth causing its interior to look more like a casserole or Kentucky than a proper tidy mouth, Betsy's teeth are perfect. They live together in peace and work in harmony. They chomp, they mash, and sometimes, because these two magnificent teeth are such a good team, they even dice their food. They are perfectly shaped and extremely happy because from birth they choose to stick together rather than fall apart and get ornery at each other and everyone else. And thus concludes the story of Betsy as well as that of the American Civil War.

EXTREME CLOSE-UP OF THE MOST PERFECT TEETH IN THE WORLD

PLEASE DO NOT LEAVE THIS BOOK OPEN TO THIS PAGE. IT'S EQUAL TO STARING INTO 100 SUNS.

NOSES OF THE WORLD

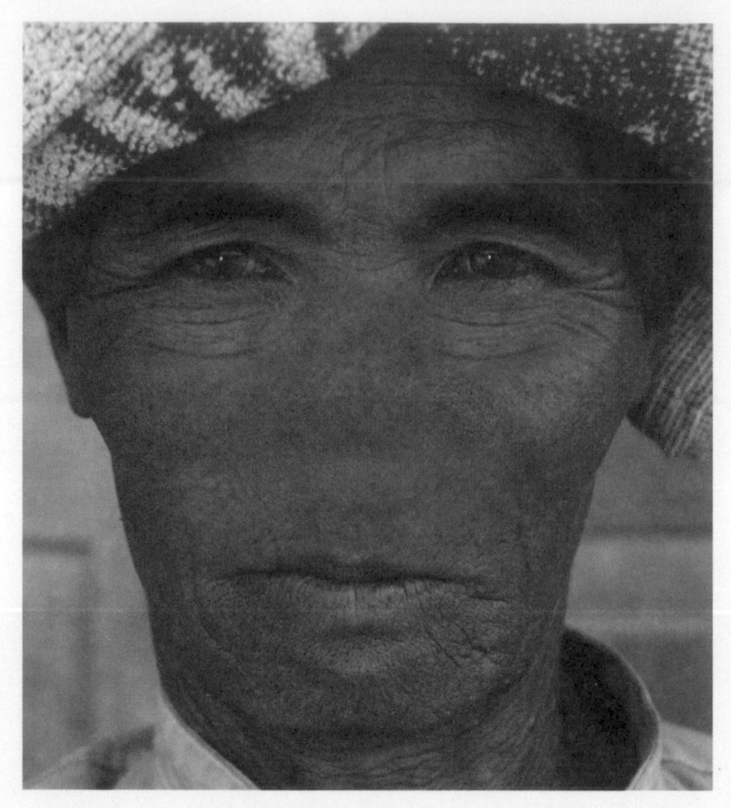

One of the Exciting Noseless People of Lower Mongolia

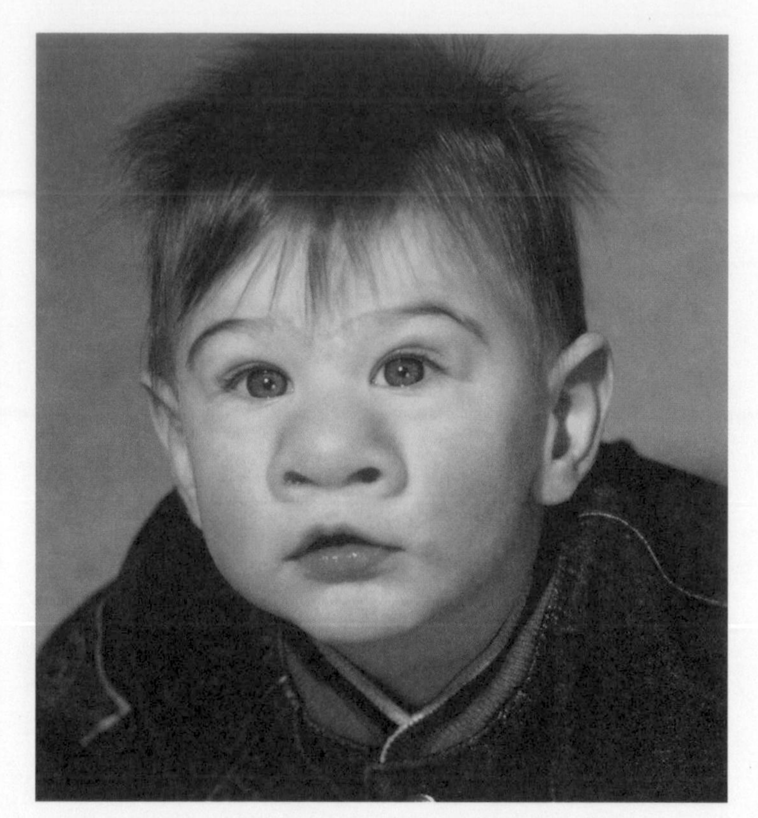

The Unsettling Round-Nosed Toddler of Ohio

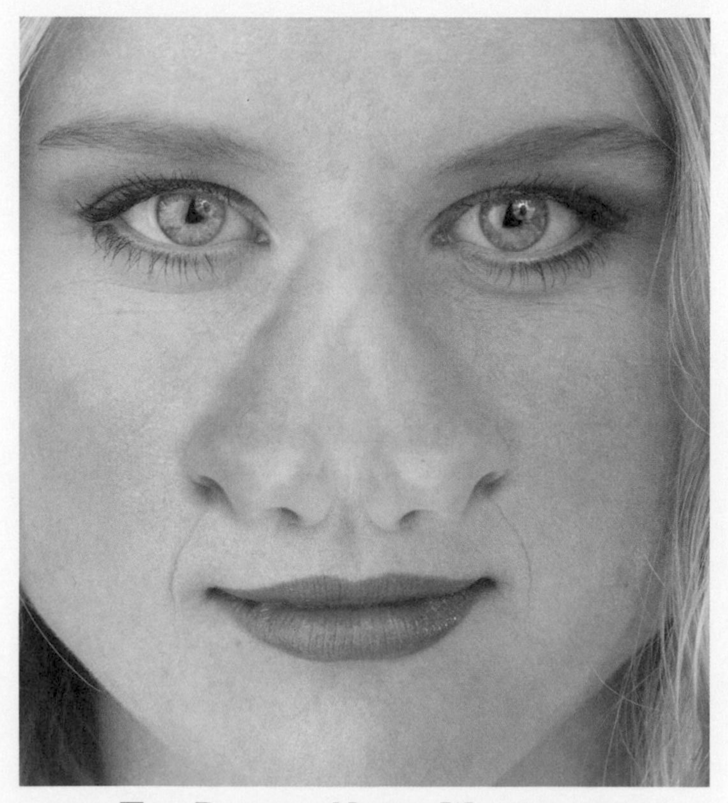

The Double-Nosed Woman of Toronto, Formerly of Vancouver

The Truffle-Sniffing Man Named Phil, of Daytona Beach

MORE NOSES OF THE WORLD

The Farmer of Midtown Philadelphia with the Hairy-Tipped Nose and Very Odd Eyes

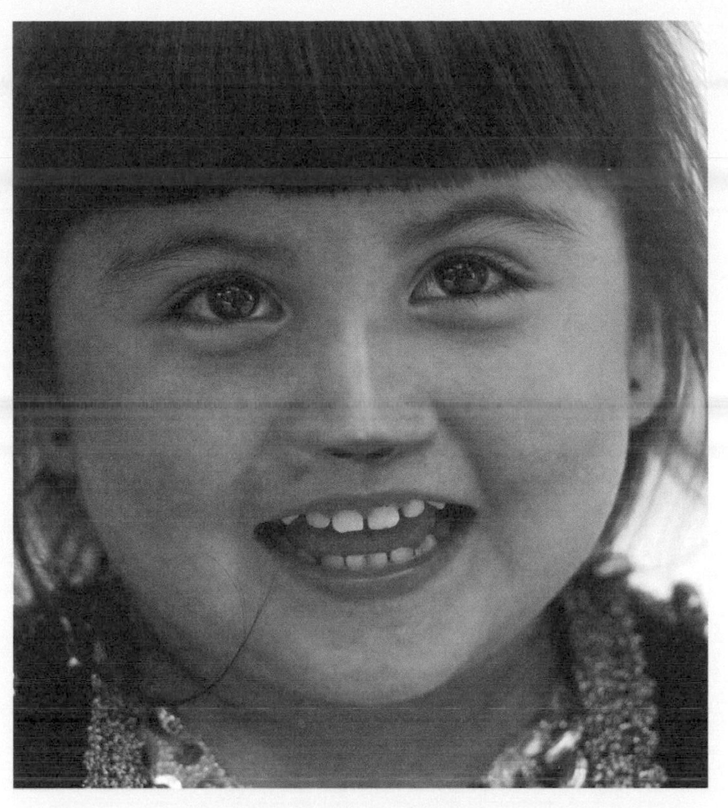

One of the Extremely Pointed-Nosed Young-Seeming People of Honduras

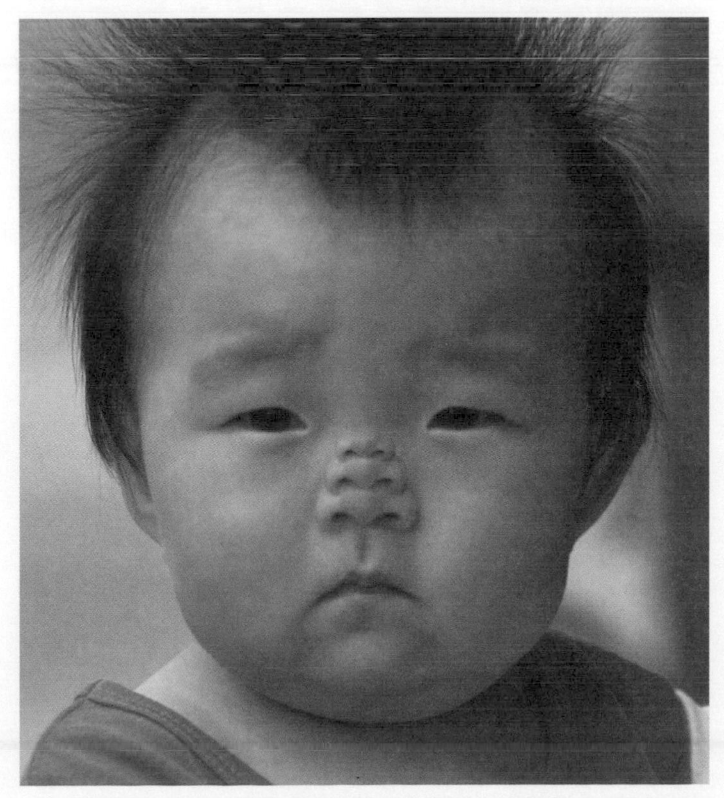

The Leader of the Hexa-Nostril Children of Lower Tibet

The Dirty-Nosed Boy of the Missouri State Fair

THE BIRDMAN OF AMES, IOWA

In the early part of this country's history, there lived a man, who was actually a woman, named Gordon, whose real name was Teresa. Teresa was also sometimes called The Birdman by those who were confused and thought she was a man, and who also thought she might be a bird. Thus Bird-man (though they did not hyphenate her name, because hyphens were invented by Alexander Haig in the summer of 1977, and this was before that).

All of this confusion about her name was caused by Teresa's very large nose, which looked like a beak, which are often worn by birds. Complicating matters were the feathers atop Teresa's head, which she wore because she was half-French and not ticklish.

Every day, Teresa would walk the streets of her hometown of Ames, Iowa, wondering why people looked at her funny, and why they called her The Birdman, and why people who did not haul things still drove pickup trucks. She also wondered, Why am I in this book, which is about Mouths, Ears, and Noses, and not Birdmen?

To which I can only offer my apologies. I, Dr. Doris Haggis-On-Whey, found a picture of Teresa in my attic, and thought it would be nice to include her in this book, though she has no scientific value whatsoever. And who are you to question me, the most towering of all scientific figures ever of all time? Look at you, in your blue corduroys and floppy hat — you cannot question me! How dare you! Sometimes I wonder why I bother. Why should I share the startling knowledge my head contains with people like you, who even your neighbors complain about. Yes they do. I heard them. They came to me for help dealing with you. It was something about how the giant ball of floss in your backyard is blocking their view. I don't see why you can't move it into the garage. You have to learn to compromise.

BENNY'S WORLD

Hi. I am Benny. Benny! That is my name.

Benny likes all kinds of games, and so do I. Sometimes we get bored when things are boring, which this book sometimes is. It's about things in your head, and things in my head sometimes bore me. I like wood better. And socks. I love socks when they're warm! But socks can't stop cars. I tried that.

On the next two pages are some games. I hope they are not boring. They're hard! Dr. Doris is calling me now so I have to go. She's gonna make me take the plastic bags off my hands, I know it.

FIND-A-WORD

Circle the words that you might hear at a dentist's office.

A A A A A A A A H
A H A A A H A A A
H A A A A A H R A
O W A O A H O O R
W O W W O O O A R
A A A A W W W R G

OPTICAL ILLUSION

Which potato is larger?

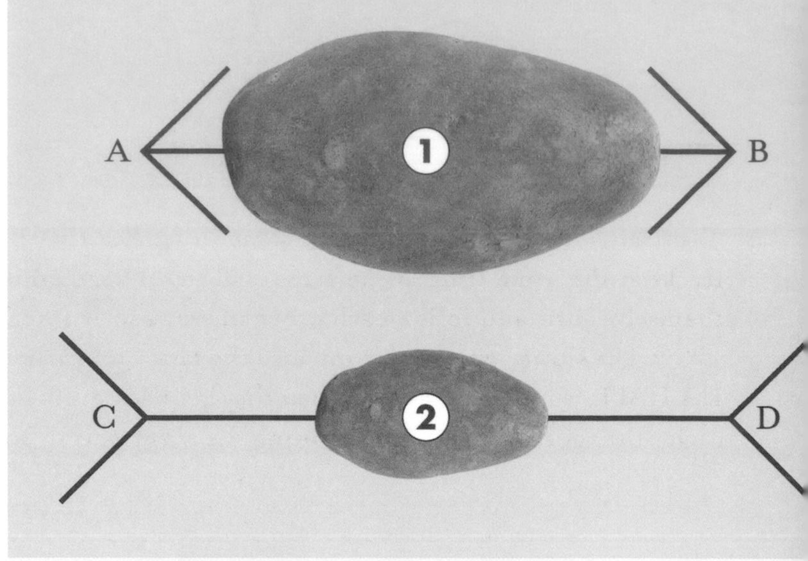

LEARN TO DRAW

Follow these simple steps, and learn how to be an artist

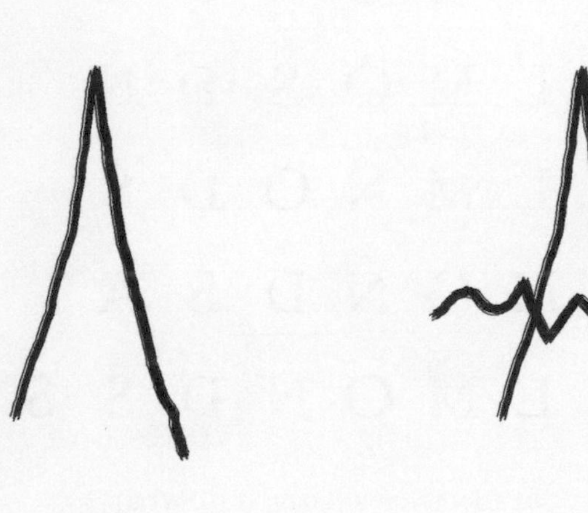

STEP 1 STEP 2

STEP 3

HOW DOES IT FEEL?

Connect the things on the left, which are things that someone might do to you, with the way they should make you feel.

1. Put your fist next to your nose, and push it, like you were punching your own nose, but really really slowly.	a. Nice.
2. Take your two biggest fingers and put them on your tongue, while running.	b. Nice.
3. Get some raisins and put them in a plastic bag and then put the plastic bag on a family member's chair. Now close your eyes while humming and pretending to blow your nose.	c. Good.
4. Find the biggest rock you can find. Now get your dog. If you don't have a dog, find a dog, or make one out of butter or lard.	d. Nice.
5. Take a large stick. Name your stick after your favorite postman. Now hide the stick in some butter or lard. After digging it out of the butter or lard, trip on it.	e. Super nice.
6. Find a tree that things often fall out of. Stand under it while singing the songs of Andrew Lloyd Webber in a gutteral Eastern European accent. Wait.	f. Pleasant.

SOLUTION: 1-C, 2-F, 3-D, 4-A, 5-E, 6-B

BENNY'S BRAIN OUCH-ER

Two trains leave the station at the same time. But they both topple on the tracks, because trains can't be on the same tracks at the same time at the same station. Where would they fit? So they topple. HA HA! Then they get up, dust themselves off, and follow each other in an orderly line. But one is going slow, and the other one is going fast. Guess what? The slower one is in front, and the faster one is behind, which means they run into each other and fall off again! HA HA! It is not their day! So then they get back on the tracks again, and they go in opposite directions, and never see each other again. Okay, now knowing the information above, what kind of sandwich should I have for dinner?

SOLUTION: Ostrich on Foccacia bread, hold the pickles.

CONNECT THE DOTS
— *WITH YOUR MIND!!*

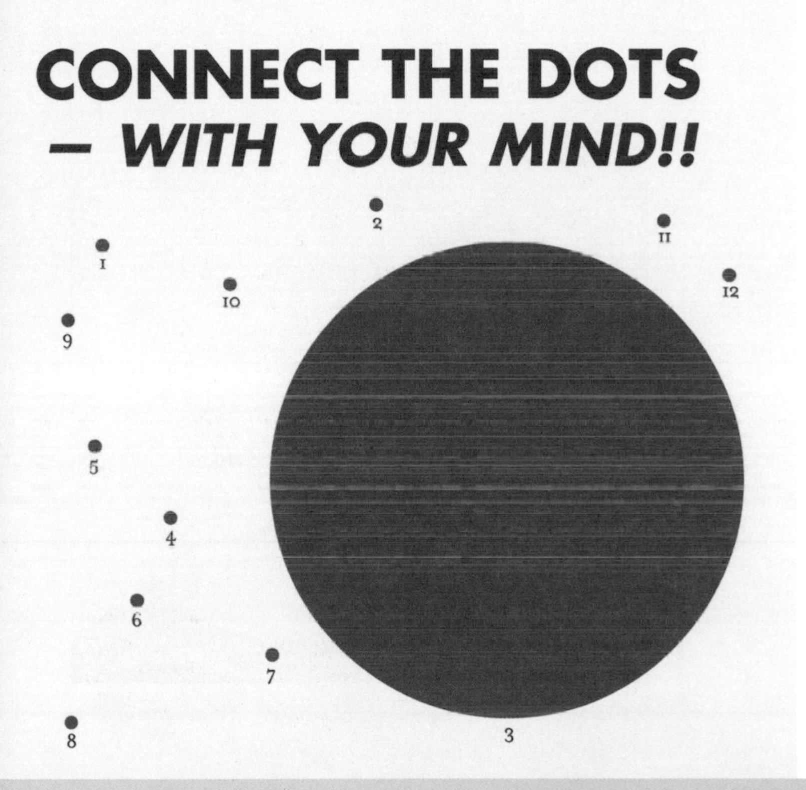

WORD SCRAMBLE

Put these scrambled words in the right order

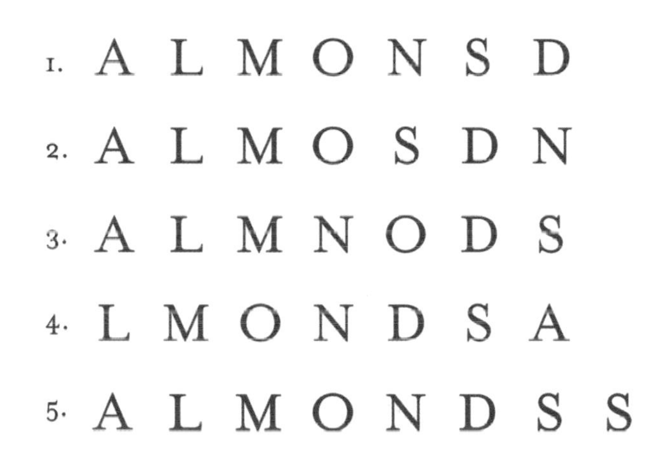

1. A L M O N S D
2. A L M O S D N
3. A L M N O D S
4. L M O N D S A
5. A L M O N D S S

SOLUTION: 1-ALMONDS, 2-ALMONDS, 3-I LOVE ALMONDS SO MUCH IT HURTS MY ARMS. I HAVE TO GO NOW.

FINDERS KEEPERS, LOSERS WEEPERS

How many differences can you spot between these two pictures?

SOLUTION: I think the birds would drink all the coffee.

GREAT SWAMP MOUTH HUNT

Can you find all seven of the mouths hidden deep inside this picture?

6

JOHN C. PACE, THE UNFORTUNATE BOY WITH THE MISPLACED FACE

John had cleaned his room, done all his chores, and even walked the dog. Now it was time to go outside and play. But as he ran down the stairs, he felt an absence around the front of his head. "Not again," sighed John and headed back into his room. "Time to go retrieve my face." On his hands and knees, John went to find what he could not see. First he blindly scoured his toy chest for his face but all he could feel was fur and hard plastic and the bones of an old wildebeest. He felt around everywhere — his closet, under his bed, in his dresser, and in his drawers — but his favorite personal attribute was gone.

"I'm never going to get to play now! What bad luck I have!" said John as he scratched his noseless nose area. "Maybe I should enlist mother for help." Then he remembered how upset she was last time he found himself faceless. They were already late for Grandma's piano recital and his face seemed very missing. So his mom did what any mother would do and left the boy in a locked room with a glass of milk and two heads of parsley. "Yeah, it would probably be better to leave her out of it," thought John.

Suddenly Sniffles, the family pigeon, flew onto the young boy's shoulder. "Hello!" cried Sniffles. "Oh, hi, Sniffles," said John. "What would you do if you couldn't find your face?" asked the boy. "Sniffles no feel good," explained the family pet, trying to get out of helping, because he wasn't a very helpful bird. "It's okay, Sniffles," said John reassuringly. "I'll just do what I normally do when things go wrong. I'll go to sleep and hope someone fixes it by the time I wake up."

And so, with that the pigeon flew back to his perch and young John C. Pace, with no teeth to brush or nose to blow, no eyes to

close or a mouth for a deep breath, merely put his head down on the pillow to await what the morning would bring.

When he woke up, he was in Russia.

The moral of the story is a simple one, which most of you have heard many times: If you lose your face, do not wake up in Russia. Why? Because the doctors of Russia are very ill-equipped to deal with face-losses. They use all kinds of old equipment, including shovels and plows, when they should be using lasers and DVDs.

Another thing about Russia: they all speak some kind of made-up language! When I went there with Benny in 1988, I couldn't understand anything they were saying. Blah-blah this, they said, and Gabba-gabba-gunk that. But they did dress well. They are extremely stylish people.

So what happened to John, you ask? Eventually he got back from Russia, and found his face in the hedges in front of his elementary school. After that, he was not only much more careful about his face, he actually transferred to another school. He grew up to be a champion Greco-Roman wrestler, specializing in wrestling very old people and trees with heavy bark.

THE TRUTH ABOUT TONSILS

Tonsils are bad news in super bold letters. I bet you think that because everyone has tonsils in their mouth, and they look so pink, that they're fine and great. I bet in that crazy head of yours you might even believe that tonsils are beautiful. What?! Are you joking, dude? Tonsils are filled with more poison than a litter of poisonous snake-frogs and that's not even the half of it! After all, can you think of anything that hides at the back of your mouth and sleeps upside-down that isn't cruel and mean? No, you can't. Let me tell you a quick story about tonsils.

In 1598 the Duke Marco of Newfoundland was a young man with a long life of gold-getting and land-seizing to look forward to. One day he was going about his usual routine of counting his money and telling servants what to do. It was a Thursday. The next day he died. Yeah, that's right, just like that. And guess what? When the police came onto the scene to investigate the murder, you know what they found out? Guess! All three of the witnesses to the crime had tonsils. The only person without tonsils was the Duke! Surprised? Well, don't be. Tonsils are wily, evil creatures and are mostly blame for all of the problems with the pop music today.

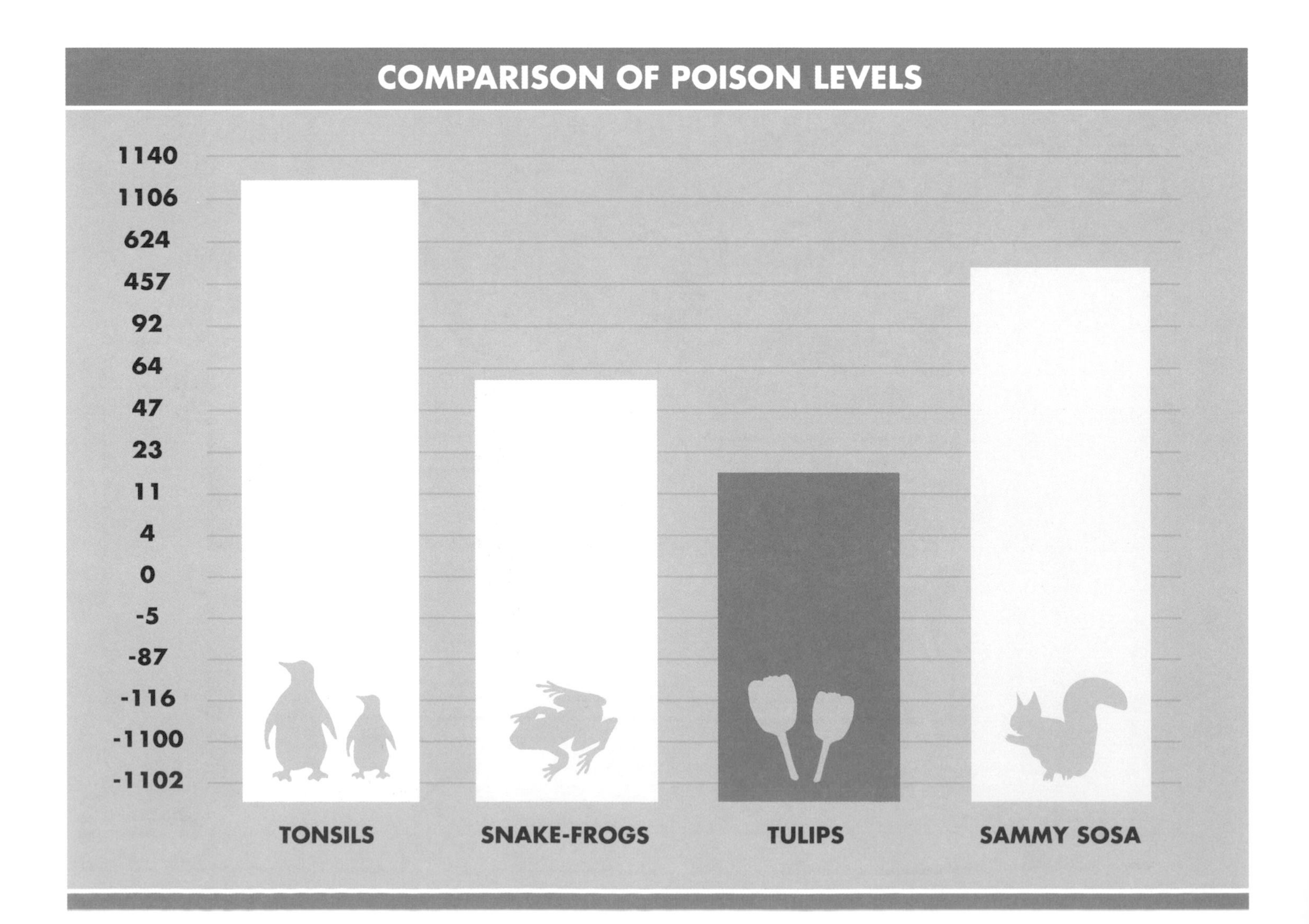

Duke Marco
1565-1598
All beware the man with tonsils

BATTLE OF THE BEST PARTS

OF YOUR DISGUSTING HEAD

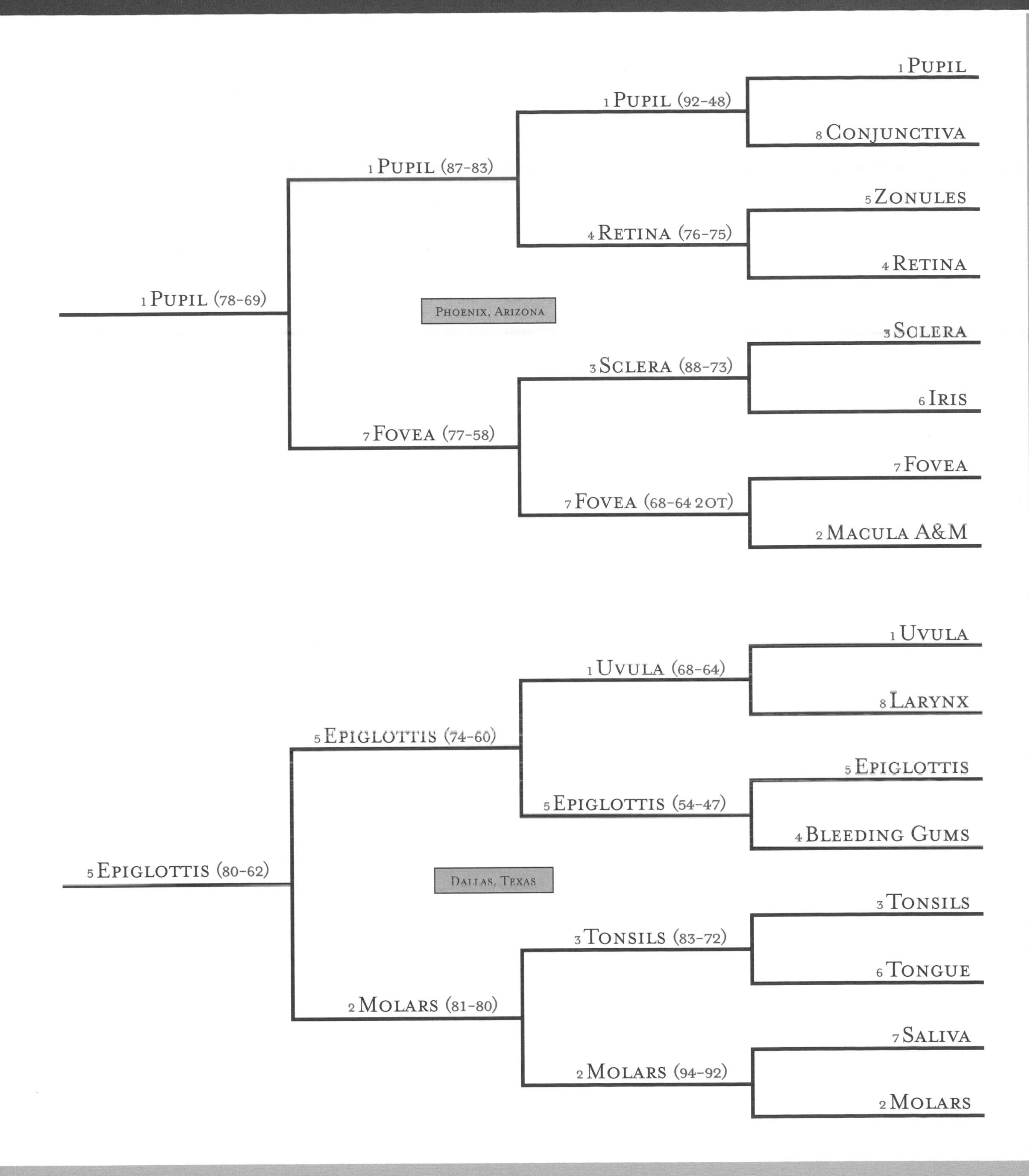

DISGUSTING HEAD CHAMPIONSHIP

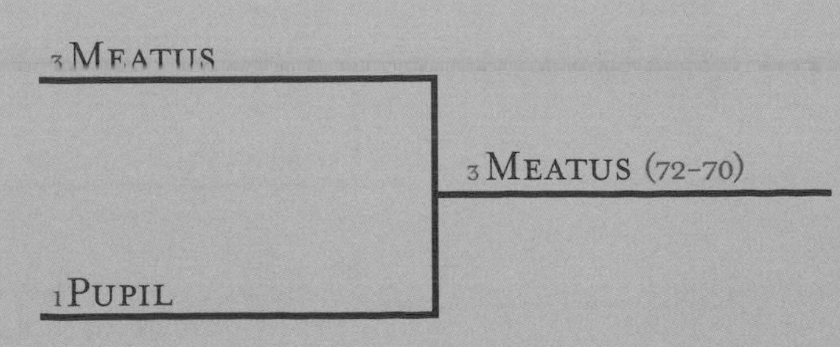

WHY YOUR EARS CAN'T HEAR YOUR PETS TALKING

For many scientists, this is the primary question of life. Indeed, for many biologists, it is the reason why they went into science in the first place. As scientists we know that our pets can think and communicate just as we do, so why can't we hear them talking? It has baffled everyone from Leonardo to Newton to Hawking. But it does not baffle Dr. Doris Haggis-On-Whey. The answer is simple: your pet is a mumbler.

While most researchers guess that it has something to do with human ears not being on the same frequency as our pets', or that they simply speak a different language, I know better. Our pets actually do speak English — and Cantonese — and do so with impeccable grammar. The only problem is that they mumble. Everything they say is sort of growled under their breath, making their words all but impossible to hear and understand unless you're right up next to their mouths. And when you're right up next to their mouths, they never talk. They just sit there, licking and chewing and thinking of all the things they're going to say once you're out of earshot.

DON'T TRUST MONKS TO GET YOU A GOOD PHOTO OF A PET OR TO PUT TOGETHER A NICE CHART ILLUSTRATING HOW A PET TALKS IN A MUMBLY WAY

Readers of *Giraffes? Giraffes!* will remember that I had some problems in that book with certain groups of monks, who were supposed to give me a nice drawing of former Secretary of Agriculture Pendleton, but who couldn't do it because they were very unsanitary. I walked into about ten monasteries, all of them in the Maine and New Hampshire area, each time just looking for some clean monks who could draw a man with one leg much shorter than the other. And you know what I found, again and again? Really unclean monks! There was no attention paid to sanitariness at all. I was aghast. What happened to the pride? There was a time when monks really took pride in their appearance, kept their fingernails clean and kept food off of their legs. But no more. I had to go to a non-union monastery to find a clean monk who could draw. It was a huge hassle. Which brings me to this page. This page was supposed to feature two things: a nice picture of a pet, and a nice chart which would help illustrate what mumblers pets are. So again I went out on the road, looking for a sanitary monk. And three weeks and 2,340 miles later, I was still looking! So I apologize for the lack of a nice chart and a nice picture of a pet. It wasn't my fault! Write to or call your local monastery and ask them what happened to being clean. Just ask them and see what they say.

WHICH TEETH WILL BITE?

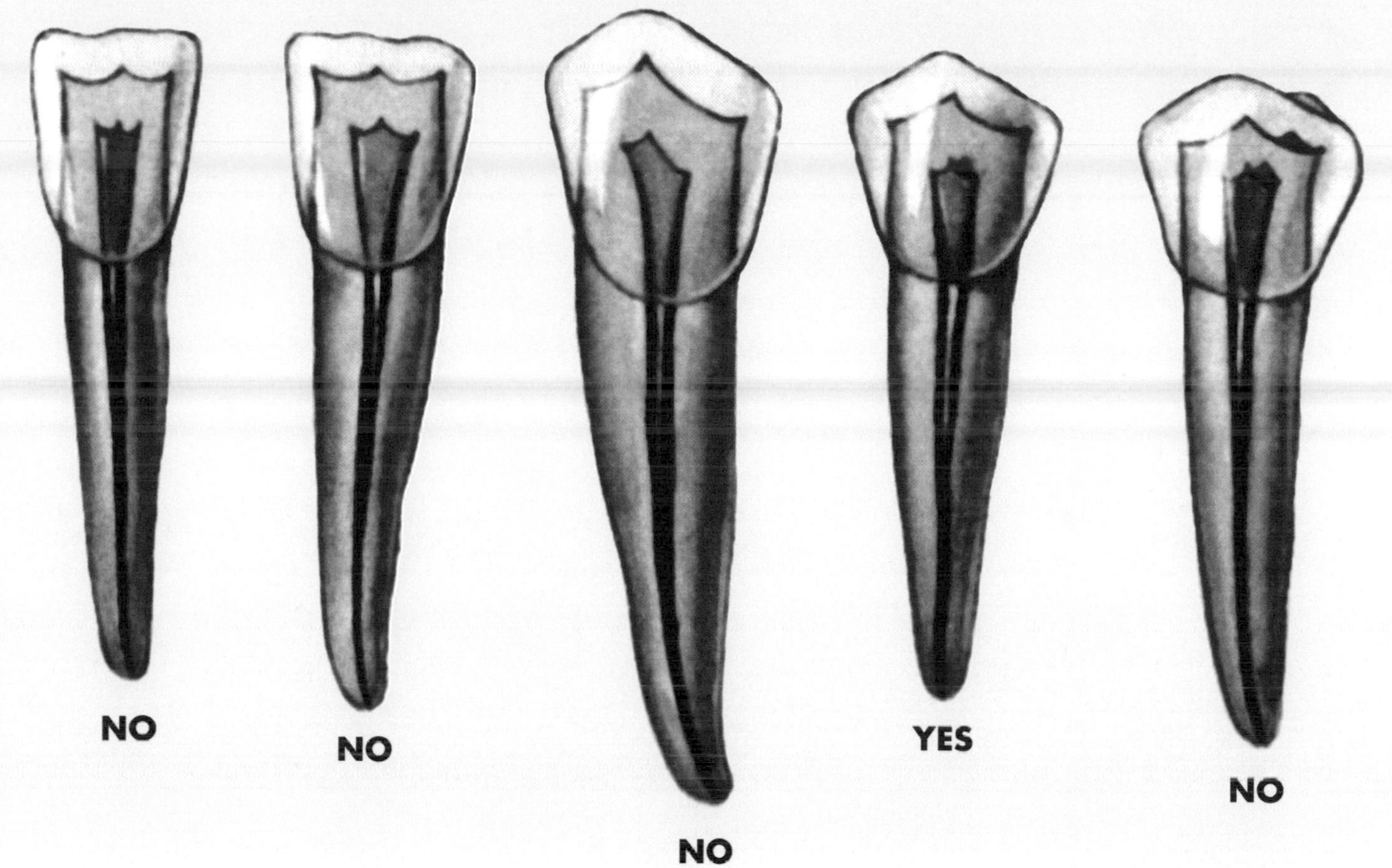

WHOSE MOUTH DO YOU HAVE?

Your father's

Your mother's

Chester A. Arthur's

HOW TO CHOOSE THE BEST TONGUE FOR YOU

So you've decided to finally go and buy yourself a tongue. I commend this decision. Many people go through life without a tongue, thinking that tongues are unnecessary, a thing of the past. Well, hogwash. I have a good deal of proof that tongues make life more enjoyable for all animals except for gerbils, who of course don't need tongues because why would a gerbil need a tongue? Please, try to keep up.

But for the rest of us mammals, tongues are essential for our sense of well-being and for wiping food from the sides of our mouths when we find ourselves without napkins or hands, such as when we are knitting.

How does one choose the right tongue? Follow the guidelines below.

1. THINK HARD ABOUT WHAT YOU WANT IN A TONGUE. What sort of tongue are you really looking for? A happy-go-lucky tongue who can make you laugh and who likes to experience new things? Or a mellower sort of tongue, one that will listen to your problems and offer a shoulder to cry on when you're looking to cry on the shoulder of a tongue?

2. LOOK FOR A GOOD VALUE. Tongues can cost anywhere from $8 to $11.50. What accounts for this huge disparity in cost? Talk to your local retailer about what separates one tongue from the next. Are the tongues made in Europe truly better? Should you splurge on one that's reinforced with steel cables? Don't throw away your money on fancy brands and high-pressure sales techniques. Make sure you're getting what you need at a reasonable price.

CARING FOR YOUR NEW TONGUE

Congratulations on your recent tongue purchase. I expect that you and your tongue will have many great adventures together. Here's a great way to start off on the right foot with your new tongue: take those greedy hands of yours and do something useful for once, like knitting your new tongue a cap or cozy.

MATERIALS NEEDED

Schoeller Stahl Fortissima Socka [75% wool, 25% nylon]; color #21,413: orange
Steinbach Wolle Strapaz [80% wool, 20% nylon]; color #34,872: burgundy
3 sets Chicken Drumsticks size #2/2.75 mm double point (set of five)
4 healthy Venus Flytrap houseplants
1 pair flame retardant eye goggles

3. AVOID TONGUES MADE WITH STRAW, DIRT, OR MORTAR. There was a time when all tongues were made with these archaic materials, but those days are over — or should be. There are much better ways to make a tongue now: fiberglass, titanium, rubber... the list goes on. Tongue technology is moving quickly, innovations abound, and you need to look for tongue construction that will last.

4. YOUR TONGUE DOESN'T NEED TO BE ABLE TO VACUUM. Sure, there are all kinds of tongues on the market that feature radios, cellular phones, and DVD capabilities. There are even tongues that can program the lights in your house! But do you really need your tongue to do all of these things? Sometimes, with all the bells and whistles, we forget what a tongue is supposed to do, which is remove beef jerky from between your molars.

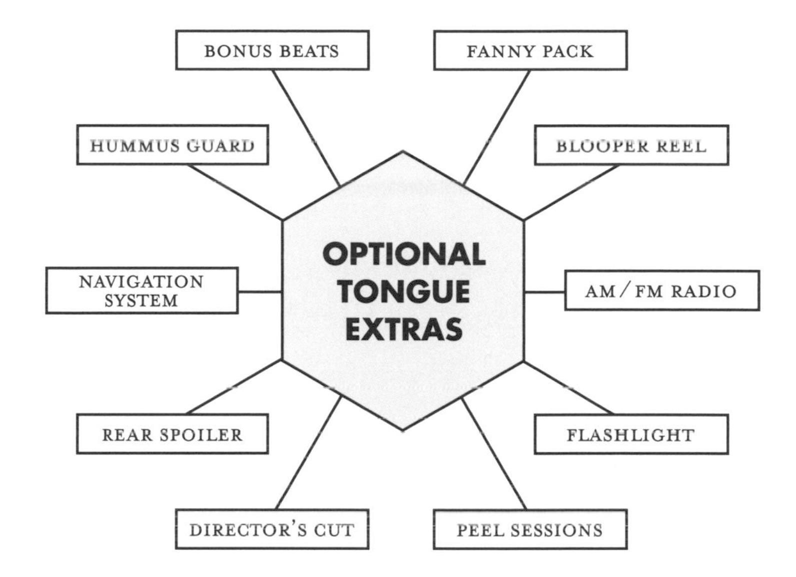

5. CHOOSE A STYLE THAT'S RIGHT FOR YOU. There are striped tongues, and tongues that look great in high heels. Don't be taken in by the latest trends and highest fashions. This tongue has to work for you every day, so make sure it's sensible. Do you really want a tongue that only seems to look right in formal settings? No. You need a tongue that's just as comfortable at a family barbecue as it is at a White House dinner honoring popular country-music pioneers Sawyer Brown.

KNITTING DIRECTIONS:

ROW 1: TRY TO NOT SCREW THIS UP.
ROW 2: K.
ROW 3: K 1 TBL, P17, SLP 1.
ROW 4: K 1 TBL, K8, DD, K8, SLP 1.
ROW 5: K 1 TBL, K8, P CENTER STITCH, SLP 1.
ROW 6: K 1 TBL, K9, DD, K9, SLP 1.
ROW 7: BREAK TIME: 2 RC COLAS.
ROW 8: K 1 TBL, K9, DD, K9, SLP 1.
ROW 9: K 1 TBL, K8, DD, K8, SLP 1.
ROW 10: K 1 TBL, K9, DD, K9, SLP 1.
ROW 11: KNITTER'S CHOICE.
ROW 12: K 1 TBL, K8, DD, K8, SLP 1.
ROW 13: JUST LIKE ROW 3, BUT BACKWARDS.
ROW 14: K 1 TBL, K7, DD, K7, SLP 1.
ROW 15: K 1 TBL, K9, DD, K9, SLP 1.
ROW 16: FINISH ALL THE DARK MEAT.

FINISHING:

Has it been an hour yet? If so, remove the yarn from your drumsticks, and sit on it for the next two hours. When you get up, you will have made a beautiful present for your new tongue.

MADAGASCAR

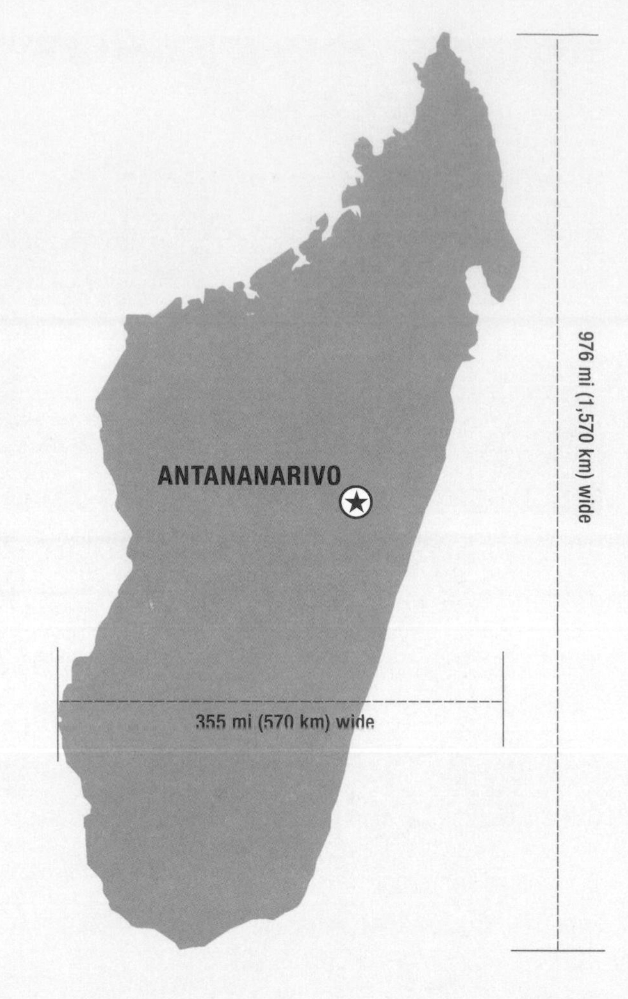

(md´´gs´cär) Madagascar, officially **Democratic Republic of Madagascar**, republic (1995 est. pop. 13,862,000), 226,658 sq. mi. (587,045 sq. km.), in the Indian Ocean, separated from East Africa by the Mozambique Channel. Madagascar is probably the world's fourth-largest island, if you're not counting Swaziland, which isn't an island and by most accounts no longer exists. Madagascar also includes many small surrounding islands, including Juan de Nova, Europa, the Glorioso Islands, Tromelin, and Bassas da India. The capital is Antananarivo — this is the country's largest city, too. The country is divided into six provinces, all of which are named Barry.

KEY FIGURES

POPULATION: 16,062,000

CLIMATE: Tropical along coast, world-famous mud inland, arid in south, sleet often described as "Madagascarian"

AREA COMPARATIVE: Slightly less than twice the size of Arizona, yet significantly larger than Terre Haute

AGRICULTURE PRODUCTS: Coffee, sugarcane, cloves, cocoa, rice, cassava, beans, bananas, peanuts; livestock products

EXPORTS: Whatever you need, seriously

NATURAL RESOURCES: Graphite, chromite, coal, vegemite, bauxite, salt, quartz, tar sands, zinc, non-precious stones

CURRENCY: Malagasy Franc (MGF)

LIFE EXPECTANCY: Male: 53 yrs, Female: 58 yrs

LITERACY: 75% of population

RELIGION: 50% Christian, 10% Muslim, and the rest worship ancestors and spirits

Land, People, and Government

Madagascar is made up of a highland plateau fringed by a lowland coastal strip, narrow (c. 30 mi/50 km) in the east and considerably wider (c. 60–125 mi/100–200 km) in the west. The plateau's highest point is Mt. Maromokotro (9,450 ft/2,880 m), but the Ankaratra Mts. are not far behind, reaching c. 8,670 ft (2,640 m). The plateau was at one time rich with forests, grasses, and animal life, but now it's pretty much stripped bare. A national park, also called Barry, was established in 1997 to protect the island's lemurs, rare orchids, and other unique wild species. A series of lagoons along much of the east coast is connected in part by the Pangalanes Canal, which runs (c. 400 mi/640 km) between Farafangana and Mahavelona and can accommodate small boats. The island has several rivers, including the Sofia, Betsiboka, Manambao, Mangoro, Tsiribihina, Mangoky, and Barry.

Aminals

Madagascar is home to many species of lemur, which is a small aminal that looks like a cross between a monkey and a squirrel. However, the lemur is not to be confused with the squirrel monkey, which is a very different aminal, and one that likes to grow small vegetables and repair old radios. There are many, many other species of aminals on Madagascar, but they are all named Barry.

Climate

Madagascar is known for its mud and its sleet.

Relation to Your Head (Disgusting)

What, you may be asking, is this stuff about Madagascar doing in this book, when everyone knows that your head is disgusting and that many creatures in Madagascar do not have heads? The answer to that question is too difficult to explain. I could explain it, but you would be staring at me, drooling and bug-eyed, and I would lose interest.

Madagascar vs. the Los Angeles Lakers in the NBA Finals, c. 1988

Wow, that was a great game. Orlando Woolridge, who wasn't even playing for the Lakers, had a great game. As did Dan Quayle, the Vice President of the United States. He was a terror on the boards, and also very good at stealing the ball and other things. In the audience that night was the cast of *That's the Roof of My Mouth!* and they enjoyed the festivities immensely.

WHY DOES MY MOUTH HATE EATING ICE SO MUCH?

Your dentist will tell you it's because you might have some cavities but that's only a small part of the truth. The fact of the matter is that your mouth is extremely wet. It is alarming how wet and moist and watery your mouth is all the time. Ice, on the other hand, is just frozen liquid. It is stuck in its form and it is very content in being frozen. Your mouth looks at this peacefully nonmoving entity and it ANGERS your mouth. It angers your mouth deeply. Why should I work so hard day in and day out being wet and looking really moist while he can just sit there and be frozen? Why? And so when ice comes into your mouth, your teeth grab the ice and THEY CRUSH IT! THEY CRUSII IT! TIIEY CRUSH IT AND DESTROY IT UNTIL THERE'S NOTHING LEFT! BE GONE ICE! AGHHH! GARRR! And then the gentle and stoic ice melts. It becomes water and it circulates in your mouth and quickly becomes a part of the watery system of your mouth. The ice, in its new form, finds a nice new life for itself in its new home. The ice never remembers its previous frozen life and no one tells it where it came from. But your mouth knows. Oh, yes. It does. It knows and this fact makes it feel great!

YOUR EMOTIONS

Your emotions are made in a small cupboard exactly four inches behind your left eyebrow. They are made, like anything of quality in our world, by hand. Extremely tiny hands, though. Tiny hands working on a loom. The origin and the nature of emotions is a puzzling question that has puzzled many a tough puzzle-solver. The Greeks believed in the body's four humors, the Chinese in the ying and the yang, the Wood Fairies in lighting little candles. In a way, they were all right. Here is the truth. On a giant little, tiny loom, these three small hands pull from six core traits found in every person to weave your current emotion. These six core traits are: anger, joy, sadness, upsetness, regret, and laughing. Once woven, the emotion is tested for durability and then sent to your brain to be tested out on the floor. After your brain checks off on it, it's your face's turn to make that emotion a reality. Your face will then scrunch, bend, and twist into a horrible face that will prevent everyone within a mile of you from knowing what's right or wrong with you. Sounds terrible, right? Well, just remember, without emotions you would probably be better at the President's Physical Fitness Test.

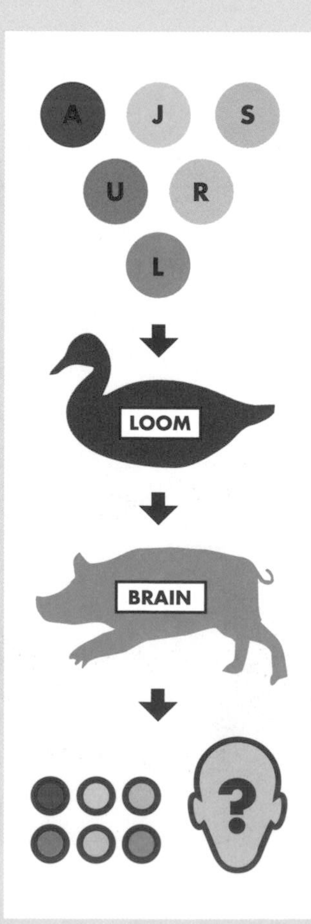

A SHORT TRIP TO THE SPACIOUS WORLD OF JOY INSIDE THE BRIDGE OF YOUR NOSE

What happens inside the bridge of your nose every day? The answer is nothing… nothing much except for the awesome and fantastic functions of AN ENTIRE WORLD! Geez. This world is called Jacob or sometimes Jacob's World and sometimes called Salt Lake City. The comparison I often draw is to the very similar world we call Mars. The difference is that Mars has no life, no water, and nothing much of interest. But like Mars, Jacob is ruled by a woman, a very small woman, a dwarf in fact, a dwarf that is a bear, a small dwarf bear, a cub. This cub, named Brenda, rules the world of Jacob from the highest peak of the great mountains of Jacob in a beautiful, picturesque little one-bedroom castle, from which she can see all of the land of Jacob. By the way, before we move on I just remembered another difference between Mars and Jacob. Mars has no children! Anyway, back on Jacob you have the queen way up there and down below you have all kinds of other stuff going on! Let me take you on a tour.

Let's be honest, this entire planet resides beneath the bony part of your nose. It's not that advanced. That's why they only have three industries: rubber bouncy balls, high-grade titanium, and red rubber bouncy balls. For shops the people of Jacob have Eric's Hardware, The Hot Hot Bakery, and D. H. Maxxy. They sell socks.

But that's not all going on in Jacob. There's also tons of fun stuff to do! Like, tree pruning! Yay! Anyway, the people of Jacob have to get back to doing stuff and we've got a book to finish. So let's leave Jacob with one more startling fact. There's no sun in Jacob but everyone there has an unbelievable tan!

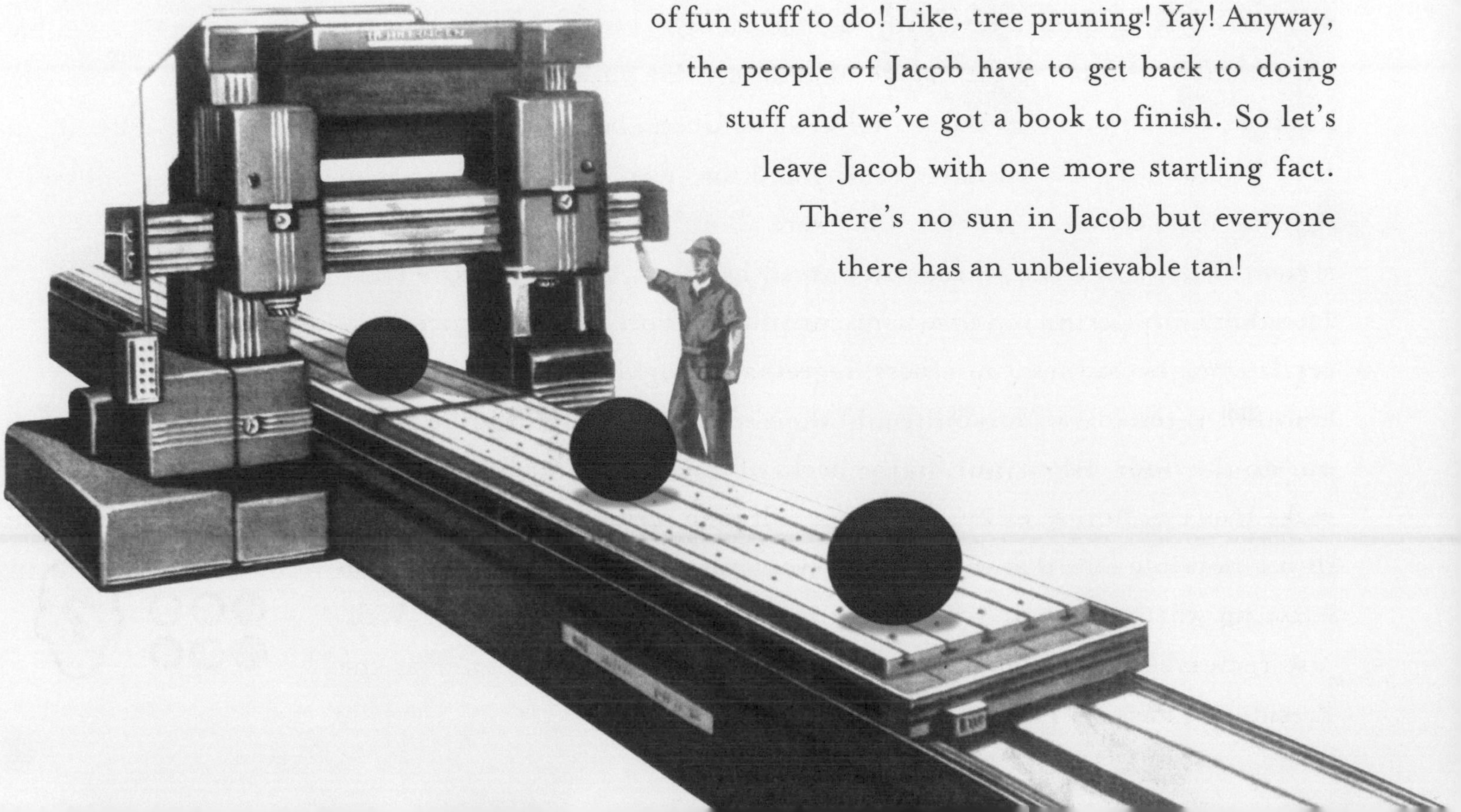

WHAT TO DO ABOUT SOMEONE NAMED OLIVER WHO CLAIMS TO BE YOUR COUSIN BUT WHO JUST GETS IN THE WAY AND MESSES UP THE SINK IN THE DOWNSTAIRS BATHROOM

This is the advice portion of this book. The advice I give you is about someone named Oliver. Let's say you are, like me, a world-conquering scientist who knows all and is feared by most. Let's say that one day you are in your lab, trying to create a new vegetable that will be bigger than a car and taste like candy. You are very busy, very deep in concentration. Suddenly there is a barking sound. You don't look up, because you figure it's Tuesday, when your husband Benny dresses up as a poodle. But then you realize it's not Tuesday, it's Saturday, and you haven't showered in eight days. Then you realize that there is someone else in your lab. This person is not Benny.

"Hello, Doris," this person says. The person's voice sounds like a person's voice, but it's coming from what looks like a small ugly dog. "I am your cousin Oliver," the dog says. "My mom, your aunt Edmund, sent me here to spend the summer and to learn everything I can from you. Isn't that exciting?"

Let's say that you do not find this exciting. Let's say that you soon remember this cousin Oliver, because he looked different from most members of your family, in that he looked exactly like an English springer, a breed of dog known for their criminal tendencies. Let's say that you never liked this cousin too much, because he always smelled of tuna and wanted to talk about women's volleyball. And just as you're remembering this, Oliver will say:

"Hey, Doris, what do you think about what's going in women's volleyball? I sure like women's volleyball..." Then he continues like this for a while, until you sneak out of the room when he's licking himself.

Let's say that you are a scientist with much work to do, hundreds of reference books to write, and you cannot have distractions like this! Let's say that you have tried to shake free of this Oliver in many ways, including putting him out with the recycling. Let's say that nothing has worked, and all you want is a little peace and quiet, so you can change the very nature of the world and its knowledge?

Let's say that you thought of one thing that might make a difference, and that is if you could get a few hundred thousand signatures on a petition, maybe Congress or the king of England or whatever could force Oliver to leave the Isle of Air and go back to his mother Edmund, who is only slightly better looking than Oliver and lives in the suburbs of Akron, OH.

Please sign the petition postcard below and send it to your local representative or king or queen:

DEAR REPRESENTATIVE / ROYAL PERSON ____________________,
(CIRCLE ONE)

Give Dr. Doris a break! She didn't ask for Cousin Oliver to come and stay with her! And for a whole summer? That's insane! He stinks of tuna and wants to talk about volleyball played by women. I ask you to pass lots of laws and make many pronouncements to make Oliver go home, or at least live in a small red house in the backyard. If you do this, I will vote for you, and give you candy at parades, and shake your hand if you shove it at me while campaigning.

Thanks,

____________________ PRINT NAME

____________________ AGE

____________________ HOMETOWN

____________________ MOTTO

____________________ OPINION ABOUT THE SECOND MATRIX MOVIE

WHAT TO DO WHEN YOUR EYES RUN OUT

You may wonder why in a book about your Nose, Mouth, and Ears, there would be a page about your Eyes, which are so unimportant that no scientists have ever even looked at them. I am wondering this, too. I think perhaps I had too many waffles today. I'm not feeling myself, so I will give you this information and then go lie down.

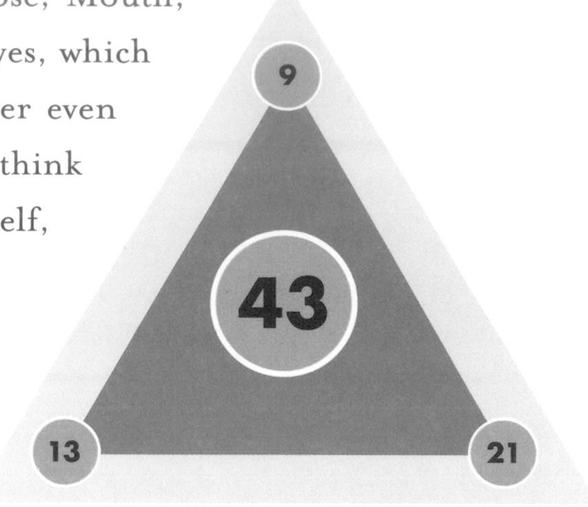

Your eyes will eventually need to be replaced. Just like your mother's and your grandfather's daughter's, your eyes, as you know them now, will one day cease to be. Fear not, though, for this is an entirely natural process. Just like the magical ages of 13, 21, and 9, I think, the age of 43 is generally recognized as the time when your eyes die. On that day you will trek down to your local eye doctor and tell him to remove your eyes and give you a fresh pair. Simple as that. How do the doctors do it? Well, with scissors, of course! And glue. Scissors and glue. Oh, and an eye-popper device that works much like a gumball machine, or probably most accurately like a vacuum.

WHO LIVES IN YOUR EYE

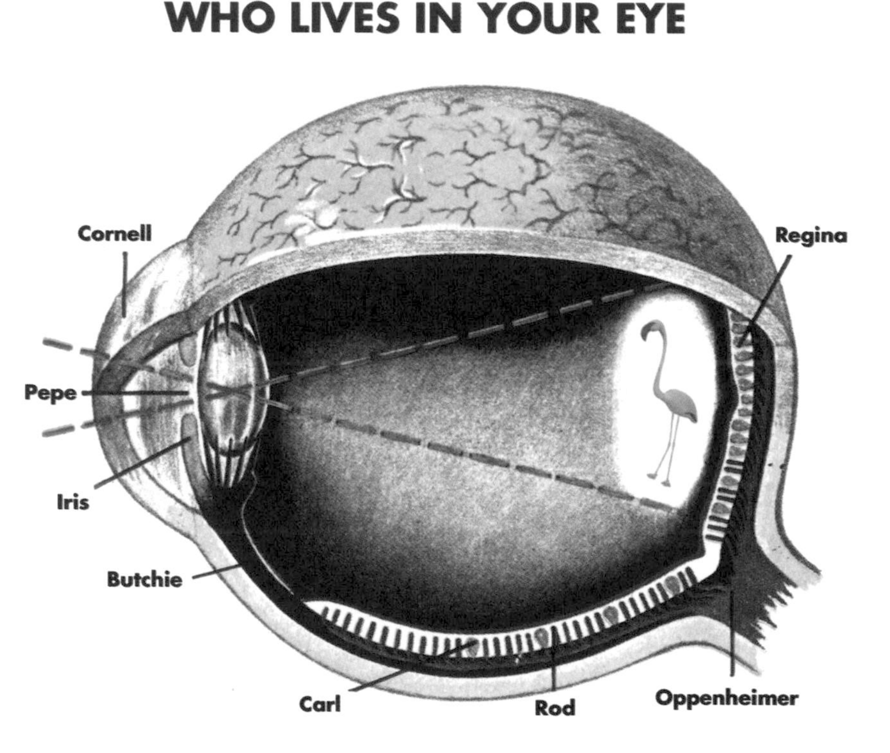

In a few seconds, the eye doctor sucks out your old set and pops in a fresh, sticky new pair. Then he or she sends you home and makes you watch TV for fifteen hours straight. Then, following doctor's instructions, you gargle mayonnaise and shortly thereafter you're good to go. But this whole process will not happen to you for a number of years. Many, many years down the line. Half a lifetime. That is, unless it happens earlier. Oh my gosh, you might need them replaced right now! How's your sight? Can you read this? This? How about this?

WHAT YOUR TONGUE IS ACTUALLY SAYING

While your tongue helps you to speak and communicate with the world, sometimes your tongue is actually saying something different from the rest of you.

WHEN YOU SAY...	YOUR TONGUE IS SAYING...
"Hey, Jimmy, how are those calculations coming?"	*"I'm hungry, I think for something sour."*
"Dad, I think the men at the door are here for you."	*"I am red and my moistness is something you cannot take from me."*
"What kind of a tax bracket is that going to put me in?"	*"I think I'm hungry again."*
"No. Are you joking? No way! Forget it. I would never. No. Wait, what? Really? Well I ... OK, sure. I mean, I guess I would for a dollar."	*"Soon one of us will be lifted and made to feel light."*

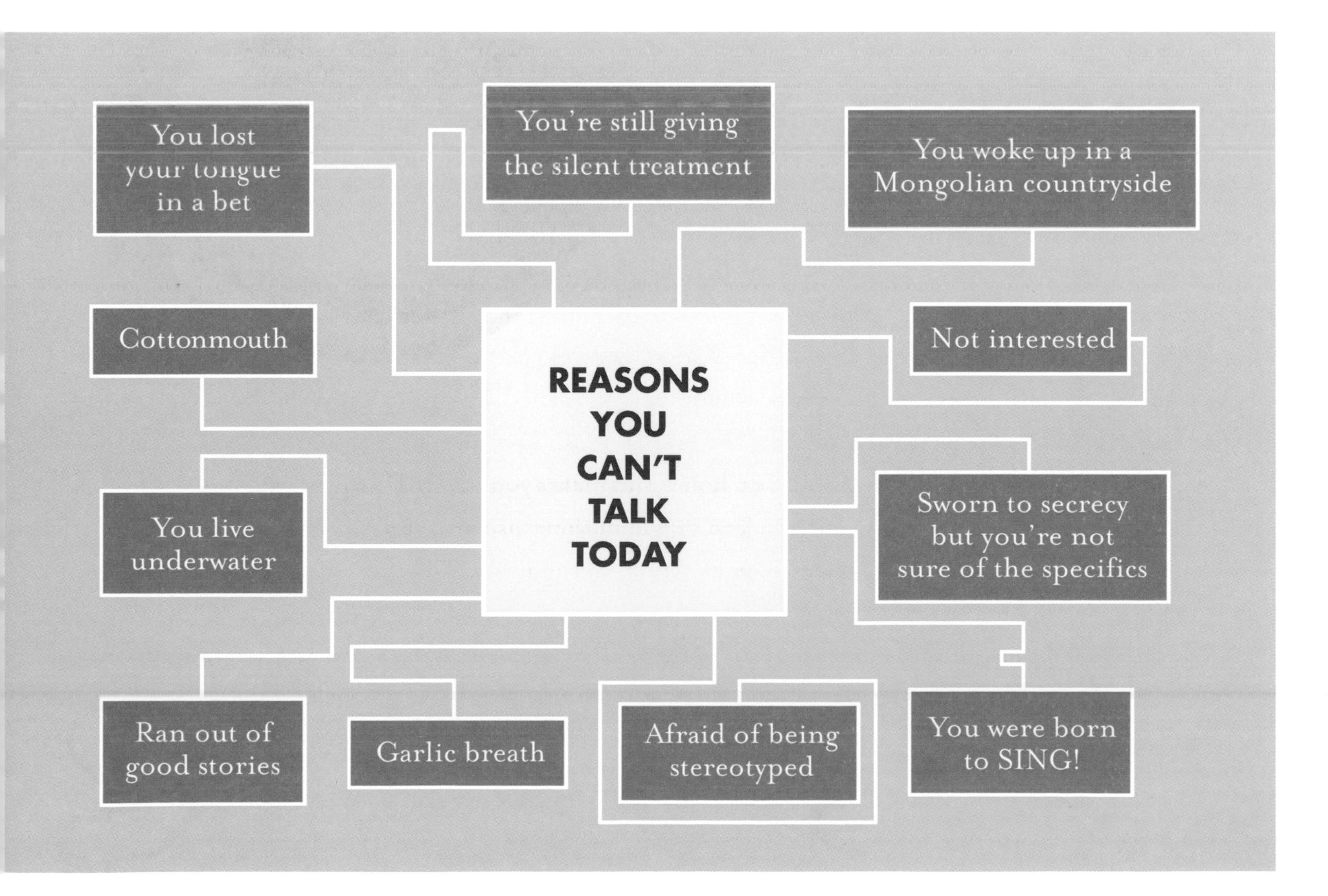

STOP BRUSHING, SCRUBBING, BLOWING, AND Q-TIPPING — BEFORE IT'S TOO LATE!

If there is one thing you must get out of this book, it is this: you should immediately stop "cleaning" your teeth, ears, and nose. We all know that from a young age, you are told to rub a hard bristled stick all over your teeth, and to put a plastic string between your teeth, pull it down until it makes your gums bleed, and then twist it around. I mean, did cavemen have toothbrushes, and floss? Certainly not. Then why do these so-called "dentists," who are actually failed soccer coaches, insist on your doing these inhumane things? I mean, how do you think all that makes the teeth feel? How would you like to be scrubbed with a huge bristly brush? To be soaked in foamy paste that tastes like window cleaner — I mean mint? Remember the cavemen!

About nose-blowing: who was the imbecile who thought of this? Honestly, as a scientist, this kind of thing really is upsetting, hearing that doctors and parents are going around telling children to expel snot from their noses by blowing it out. Why would you ever want anything blowing out of your body? Isn't that a bit extreme? Why must we be so harsh about the offending clutter in our noses? For decades I have experimented with a number of alternative methods of emptying one's nasal canals, and these are by far the best options:

1) *Ask* the material to leave. Most things that take up residence in your nose are well-educated and reasonable. You can calmly discuss the terms of their departure, and will probably be successful in negotiating an acceptable fee for their exit. (Note: Don't pay over $120.)

2) An anonymous note slipped into their locker. Always works.

3) Tell them you just saw Matthew Broderick at the mall. Watch them run!

Finally, I would like to address this notion that we need to clear out our ears using a little white stick with fluff on both ends. Do you know where these so-called Q-tips originated? Yes, that's right, during World War I! They were used by the French to do upsetting things to the Turks. They used to take the Q-tip-like device, hold it in front of the faces of captured Turks, and say, "One day people will be using these all over the place! Sticking them in their ears like they're harmless! Isn't that a laugh?" This wasn't that effective as a torture method, but it was educational for all involved, equally upsetting for all, and a good reason why neither the French nor the Turks use Q-tips today. The citizens of both of those great nations — Frenchland and Turkburg — do what we should all do: they give the wax $20 for a movie and let them borrow the car.

YOUR NOSE HAIRS: YOUR BODY'S FALLEN ANGELS

Like most of your body, your nose hairs were not always so ugly. In fact, they used to be downright charming. That's because back in the olden days they were well-shaped and elegant-looking. Back when they were your eyelashes. Yes, much like hula hoops or the muskrat, nose hairs are among those things of life forever condemned to live in knowledge of a former greatness that will never be achieved again. As you may know, your eyelashes die often. They die, they fall, and then they get stuck on your face. Then, of course, someone whom you may or may not like reaches over and grabs the dead thing off your cheek, and then, like a jerk, he or she sticks it in your face until you blow it and make a big wish. And so you do. And that's that. It's really a ridiculous custom and I'm doing everything in my power to end it.

NOSE HAIR GROWTH

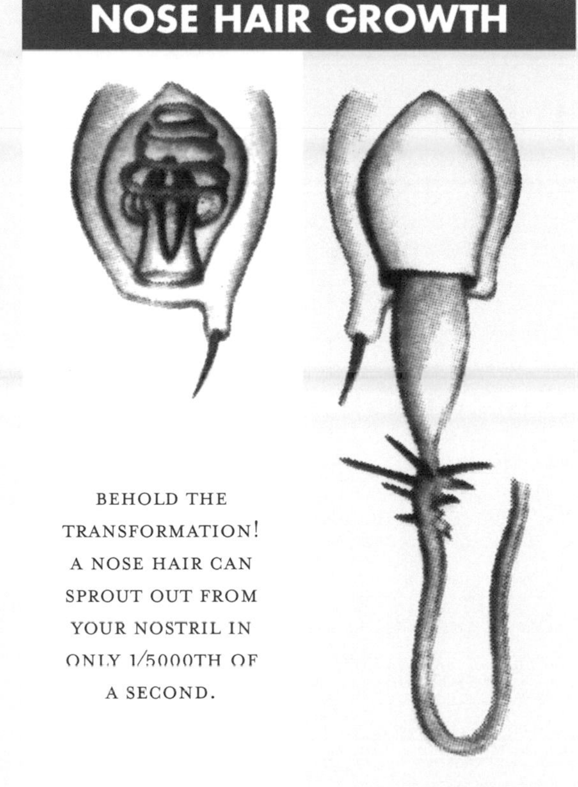

BEHOLD THE TRANSFORMATION! A NOSE HAIR CAN SPROUT OUT FROM YOUR NOSTRIL IN ONLY 1/5000TH OF A SECOND.

What happens next? In a process called distill-osmosisfication, your ugly, dead eyelash that you thought you blew out of your life forever rides the winds of fate right back into your nose. In that dank and humid world inside your nostril, your eyelash suddenly finds itself surrounded by all the ghosts of eyelash lore. Every single black, perfectly formed eyelash it ever knew and even ones before its time give halfhearted hellos to the eyelash, welcoming the new arrival to the last home it will ever know. For like the Greek afterlife, or New Mexico, your nose is a final resting ground that knows no exceptions.

No matter how beautiful or well-regarded you might have been as an eyelash, those days are no more. A person has no respect for anything in his or her nose. As a nose hair you are shunned. Shunned for getting stuck with boogers, for adding to congestion, for sticking yourself out to say hello during a big date. You are hated. You are the reverse metamorphosis, from butterfly to really ugly-looking caterpillar. So live now, great eyelash, for your time in the sun is short, and the memories must last a lifetime in a cave of envy.

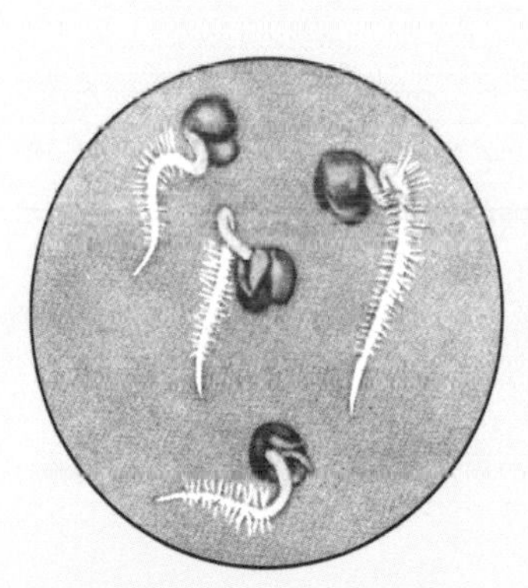

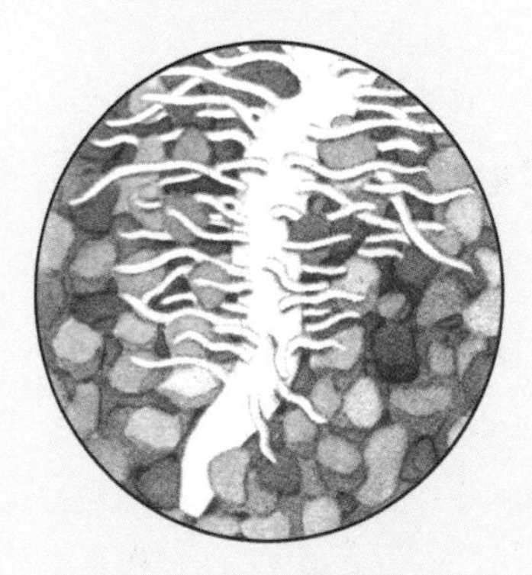

THE HORRORS OF DISTILL-OSMOSISIFICATION AS SEEN THROUGH THE WORLD'S NINTH MOST POWERFUL MICROSCOPE.

THE STORY OF YOUR SUB-MAXILLARY GANGLION

In your mouth you have a sub-maxillary ganglion and that's pretty much all you need to know. Except you also need to know it is extremely small but also extremely irritable, so LEAVE IT ALONE! Your sub-maxillary ganglion is the smartest thing in your body. Actually, that's not true. It's the second smartest. No, no, I was right before, it is the smartest thing in your body. That's why when you have a really difficult math problem to solve you ask your brain for help, but when your mouth has a problem it asks the sub-maxillary ganglion. This may seem a little strange but to be frank your mouth has much harder problems to solve than any stupid math question.

THIS IS NOT A RIDE AT SIX FLAGS GREAT AMERICA

Your sub-maxillary ganglion organizes all the duties of your teeth, keeps your tongue in line, monitors your breath, makes sure your gums are bleeding and also, on her lunch break, your sub-maxillary ganglion helps monitor your heartbeat. Sometimes it even helps your heart pump blood! And to think you didn't even know what it was! Without your sub-maxillary ganglion you would be close to helplessness, and more importantly, you would have some strange scarlet-like fever. Or maybe it was shingles.

What can I do to thank my sub-maxillary ganglion, you ask? Luckily, all she — for all sub-maxillary ganglia are female — requires is that you talk to her from time to time. She enjoys talking about a number of things. Actually, she really doesn't like talking. You would probably bore her, so don't bother. She loves movies, though. Go rent something nice, perhaps starring that adorable Reese Witherspoon. But nothing scary. Your sub-maxillary ganglion doesn't like to be scared. Has Reese Witherspoon been in a scary movie? If so, don't rent that movie. Rent something nice.

YOUR TONGUE: YOUR BODY'S OWN MOOD RING

The color of your tongue can tell you a lot about your state of mind. Match your tongue's current color with one below to find out your present disposition.

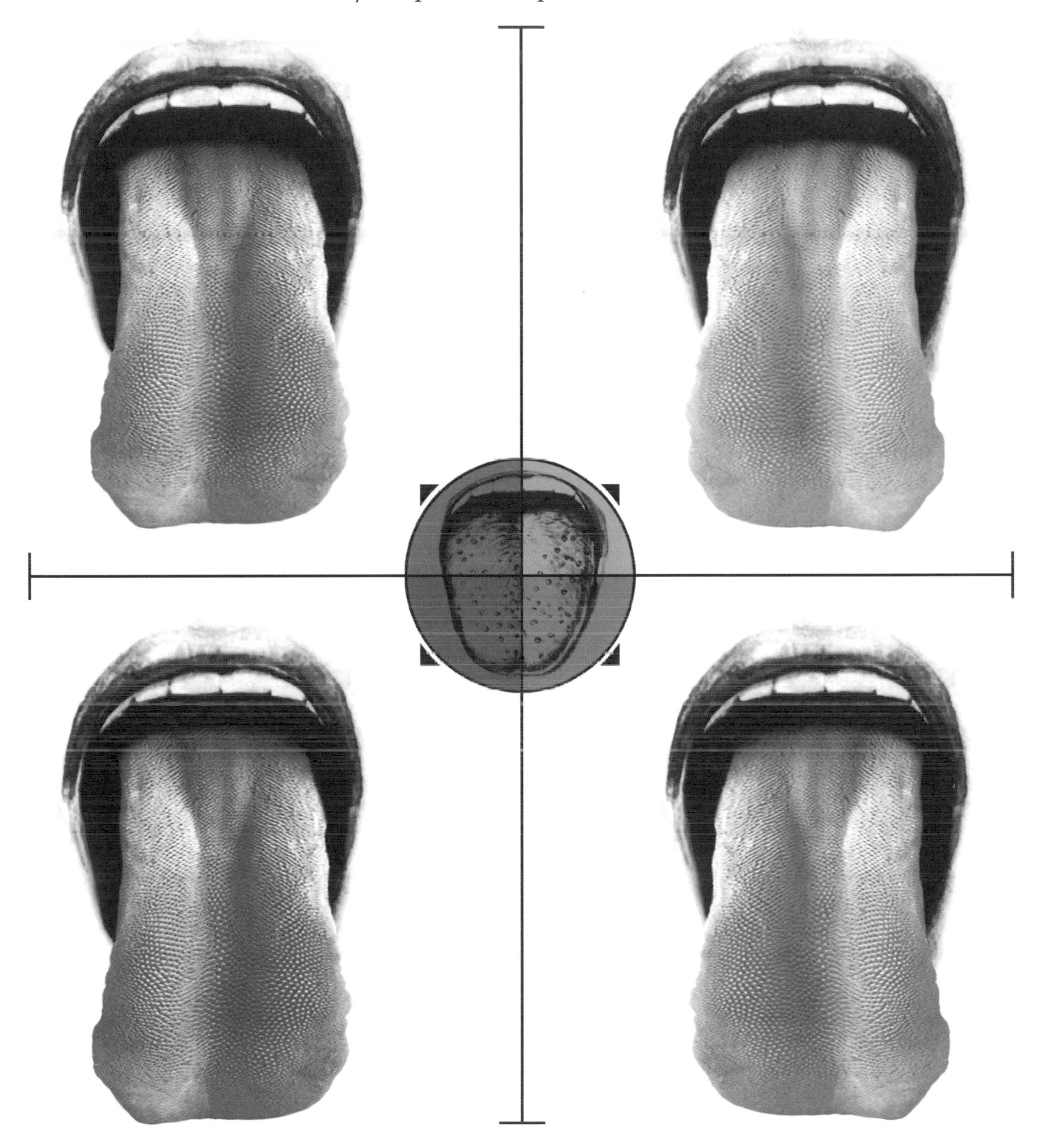

ORANGE: You're full of joy and laughter! You're in the world's oyster and there's a free buffet. Gorge yourself, because people love you! The sun says, "Good day." However, there's a high chance you'll be beat up today.

GREEN: You're tired but only nap-tired. Beware of post-nap grumpiness. Drink plenty of wet fluids and try to be still. And stop cursing under your breath!

PURPLE: Congratulations! You're German!

BLUE: You're pouty, it's true, but look on the bright side: at least you're not German.

MISSING ELEMENTS OF THE DISGUSTING HEADS OF SOME PRESIDENTS

FOUR PRESIDENTS WHO DIDN'T HAVE EARS

William Taft

Grover Cleveland

William McKinley

Calvin Coolidge

TWO PRESIDENTS WHO DIDN'T HAVE MOUTHS

Gerald Ford+

Gen. Dwight David Eisenhower

FIVE PRESIDENTS WHO DIDN'T HAVE NOSES

Abraham Lincoln

James T. Polk

James "Jimmy" Carter*

Richard M. Nixon

Alexander Hamilton**

Ronald Reagan≠

+ Some say he did have a nose.

* Some say he had two noses.

** Some say he was not actually president; nevertheless, did not have a mouth.

≠ Some say he was an actor before becoming president.

COMPOSITE PORTRAIT OF ALL U.S. PRESIDENTS

TROUBLESHOOTING GUIDE

Your head is emitting blue fluid:
You should catch this fluid in a vessel of some sort, a mason jar or bucket. This fluid is worth money! I don't know who will pay money for this fluid, but someone's gonna do it. Just keep it handy and keep your eyes open for opportunities. Man, you could be rich, if you keep emitting blue fluid.

Your nose has been removed:
Were you in Greenland? Don't go to Greenland if you don't want your nose removed.

Your mouth is redder than you want it to be — red around the edges and very dry:
This often happens during winter. Go somewhere where there is no winter.

Everything you smell smells like pig sweat:
Are you in a place where lots of pigs are sweating? Leave this place.

Everything you smell smells like pig sweat and you are not in a place where pigs are sweating. Instead, you are at home, among your family:
Wow, that's some bad luck. I'm sorry about that.

Your ears are shaped like an elf's ears:
Do you have scissors? Make sure they are very sharp. Now, you see that pointy part at the top of your ear, which makes your ear look elfin? Well, take the scissors, and then put them in a drawer. Now buy a wig. The wig should be very large, shaggy even. Put the wig on your head, so it covers the top portion of your ears. Now buy some new pants, something fancy, to go with your new wig. Now get a cool car, something long and with shiny hubcaps that spin backwards as you drive. Now put lots of rings on your fingers, and wear some shoes, huge shoes, that have, like, mini-aquariums in the heels. Eight-inch heels! You will look so cool.

Your finger has become stuck in your ear, whilst you were extracting wax from it, for some kind of experiment:
Some of the most important scientific discoveries of this century began with the discoverer's finger in her or his ear, so you should know that you are in distinguished company. Now, whilst your ear is stuffed with your finger, think about science. What kinds of things need to be discovered? Think hard about this. What sorts of things could you come up with, things no one before you has thought of? What about something with whales? For instance, maybe whales aren't so smart after all. Maybe you should look into that. What if whales only look smart? Or maybe they test well, but aren't street-smart, you know? Did you ever think about that? Well, get your finger out of your ear and start doing the calculations!

Your nose is bleeding for no good reason:
Put on a wig, like the one prescribed for those with elfin ears.

Your ears are bleeding for a pretty good reason:
Get a bucket.

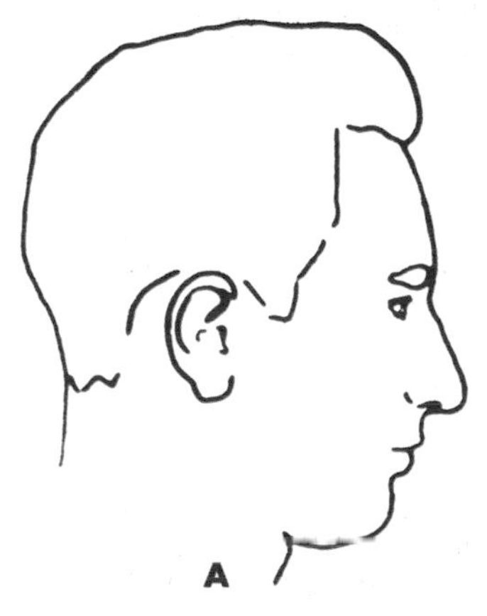

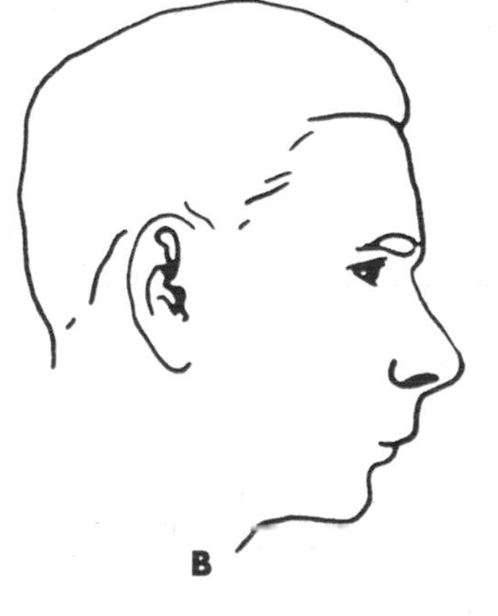

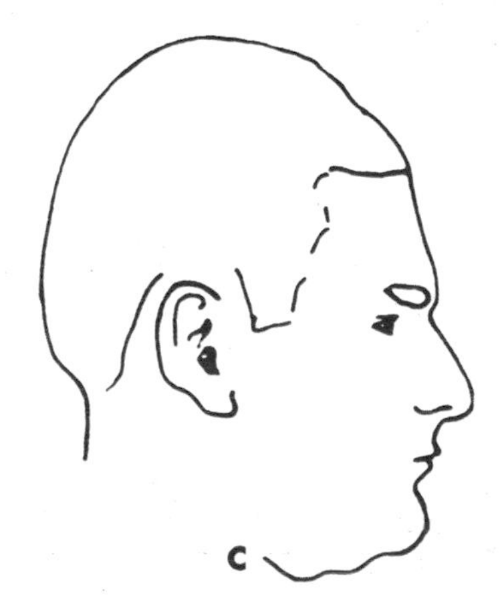

SONGS TO SING TO YOUR EARLOBES

Chorus
I think it was on the bus. It might have been at the game. I was watch-ing jai-alai, I think.
Chorus
f
But may-be I was at home, and the cal-en-dar fell out of my pock-et and in-to the couch. That could be it. What am I say-ing?
f
pp
The cal-en-dar wasn't a poc-ket cal-en-dar! It was four feet ac-ross and made of heav-y wood and Leg-os. It nev-er would have
fit in my pock-et. I don't have pock-ets that big! So any-way, I'm sor-ry I for-got your birth-day. That was lame of me.
Ped.

THE ABBREVIATED HISTORY OF DR. AND MR. HAGGIS-ON-WHEY

1935: Doris Haggis-On-Whey born in Chattanooga, Tennessee, to a husband-and-wife team of circus impersonators.

1941: At age six, Doris has discovered four new elements and has cloned a goat. Her teachers are not sure what to do with her, because she is so smart and brilliant and clever that she glows, requiring her classmates to wear special glasses and clothes to be in her presence. On her seventh birthday, she is sent to the Institute for the Advancement of Advancements, somewhere in Switzerland. There she thrives, and meets others of her extreme intellect, including two brothers named Sonny. She also diverts a meteor headed for Earth.

1953: After graduating from the IAA at age nine, Doris attends college simultaneously at the Sorbonne, Yale, Berkeley, and the University of Southeastern Russia Tech, and graduates in just over three weeks from all of them. She then spends ten years traveling the world in a plane she made herself, from balsa wood and staples. On that trip, she names all of the fish in the sea, and measures the deepest ocean floors. Bored with how easy it all is, she returns to college, this time attending Smith, where she becomes involved in theater. The picture below is from her graduation ceremony, at which she was named Smartest Person Ever to Be at Smith — Whoo! By Far, Man!

1957: Benny, born in 1934 in Thailand to a minister and his wife, grows up in Idaho, where he excels in his studies, in sports, and with the ladies. Benny is popular everywhere he goes, so full is he with charm and skill at just about everything. One day, at the urging of his classmates, he builds a hot-air balloon using a bedsheet and a hair-dryer, and flies from his Idaho home to Japan. In Japan, he buys some inexpensive electronics and returns the next day.

1962: Again bored with how smart she is and how less-smart everyone else is, Doris Haggis-On-Whey attempts to join the Navajo tribe. Though she wears her hair in a traditional way, and builds herself a teepee from the skin of a buffalo she wrestles herself, the Navajo tell her that she would be more happy living in upper Scotland, on the Isle of Air. She has not been to the Isle of Air yet, and travels there the next day, in a submarine she builds from scrap metal and cashews. When she arrives, she immediately knows that it is the right place for her — the place where she will conduct experiments, write her findings in books, and bottle some of the best jam and jelly in the Western world.

1965: After stints in the National Football League and a job with President Eisenhower, Benny decides that there is only one thing missing from his life: a woman who would soon be considered the smartest scientist ever known for all time, forever. He sets out looking for this woman, who he has heard lives on a remote island in Scotland, and who looks great in a traditional Navajo outfit. The picture above is taken while he is on his way to the Isle of Air, just minutes before the brilliant and athletic Benny is attacked by a swarm of squirrels and ferrets, and loses a good deal of his mental and physical powers. When he wakes up, the first face he will see is that of Doris Haggis-On-Whey, who will be in the forest, looking for the best place to drill to Guam. They will instantly fall in love, and Doris will bring Benny to live with her.

1971: This picture above is taken while Doris and Benny are in Antarctica, meeting the leaders of the National Penguin Council. At the invitation of the penguins, Dr. Doris and Benny travel to the polar ice caps, to talk to the penguins about global warming, and about movies they've recently seen. The penguins are big, big fans of everything Clint Eastwood does. They can't stop talking about Clint Eastwood, doing terrible imitations of him all day and night. Worse, they serve their soda warm, thinking that this makes them more sophisticated. After a few days of this, Dr. Doris and Benny can't stand it anymore, and leave on the first boat they can get, which leaves four months later.

1996: Benny spends the majority of the year sipping from this papaya.

FREQUENTLY ASKED QUESTIONS

My nose is smaller than some noses. Does this mean I am good at computers?
This means that you will go far. At least as far as Maine.

If I were to remove my ear, would I become a famous artist?
Yes, but don't use a knife, as did Vincent van Gogh. Use ointment and a Phillips-head screwdriver.

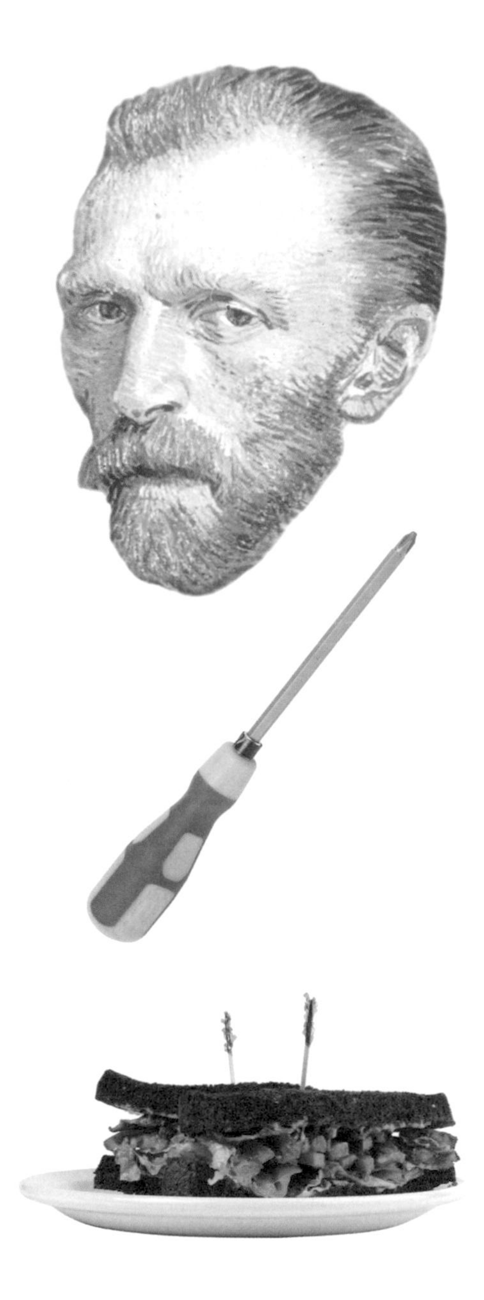

I am almost certain there are badgers living in my mouth. First of all, is this possible? And secondly, what sorts of food should I feed them?
It is entirely possible that badgers have taken up lodging in your mouth. Especially if it is wintertime, when they hibernate. As for foods they might enjoy, I would recommend any kind of club sandwich, lightly toasted. No hummus!

How many ears would it take to hear as well as a dog?
What do you mean?

I mean, how many ears would I need on my head in order to hear as well as a canine, for their hearing is known to be extraordinary.
You mean, how many regular human ears would you need on your head?

Yes, that is what I mean.
That is a ludicrous question.

Does that mean you don't know the answer?
That's not what that means.

Then what is the answer?
I'm not telling you. You're being belligerent.

I don't mean to be belligerent. I just am very anxious to know the answer to this question, for I have a big meeting coming up in Jacksonville, Florida, and everyone is counting on me to know the answer. And I started worrying that perhaps you didn't know how many ears a human would need to equal the hearing of a dog.
The answer is eleven. Eleven! Now go. Go to Jacksonville and have your meeting!

RARELY ASKED QUESTIONS

What sorts of music do ears prefer?
Synthesizer rock from the mid-eighties. There was a band called Mr. Mister, and that is your ears' favorite music.

Where do the best tongues come from?
The best tongues are grown in a farm in Cuba called El Toro, which is Spanish for "The Bull." The farm should change its name, because it no longer keeps cows and bulls. It is a tongue-farming place, and that's all.

Can you still have that operation done where they replace your tongue with a shirt?
I have no knowledge of this operation.

You sure? It was very popular in the seventies. They would remove your tongue, and replace it with a shirt.
No. You are wrong.

Maybe I'm getting it wrong.
Maybe you are.

It was a cardigan!
Yes, now you are correct. In the 1970s scientists from Austria and Hungary and Austro-Hungary perfected a technique whereby they could remove one's tongue and replace it with a cardigan. For many years, the children of the very wealthy insisted on having this operation when they turned 18. It was seen as a sign of status, and thousands of dollars would be spent by parents to install the finest cardigans in the mouths of their children. Everyone wanted a cardigan of cashmere, or the finest alpaca, or best yet, one made entirely of the fur of the very rare whistling dog, which was actually a bunny. The only problem with the operation, and perhaps the reason it fell out of favor, was that it made eating very difficult, and talking impossible.

My closet is full of teeth. Is this normal?
Where do you live?

I live in Sioux City.
Yes, this is normal.

Well, that is all you or anyone could possibly want to know about your head, which is disgusting. At this point, you can forget about ever knowing anything not in this book. I have to say that I am somewhat sorry for having made clear just how disgusting your head is, because many of you were not quite aware of its unbelievable hideousness, mysteriousness, and moistness. And now you are, which perhaps is not a good thing. Perhaps you would have preferred to go through life thinking that you had a nice thing resting on your neck, a nice thing full of thoughts and butterflies, instead of what it is, which is a mass of fluids and goop and things than cannot be named or mentioned. I am sorry to be the deliverer of this news, but I figured it should come from me, instead of from one of your creepy friends, who are pretty undependable, when you really stop to think about it.

Your heroes and most valued advisors,
Dr. Doris and Mr. Benny Haggis-On-Whey

Checklist for readers who think they have finished this book:

YES	NO	
☐	☐	Did I learn about the moistness of my head, and how that makes me a better person?
☐	☐	Did I learn about why my ears are so ugly?
☐	☐	Did I learn why my pets seem to ignore me?
☐	☐	Have I memorized all of the presidents who did not have ears?
☐	☐	Did I read this book slowly enough to last as long as possible, thus prolonging the greatest joy of my young life?
☐	☐	Did I figure out a way to make the world a better place, given what I now know about the disgustingness of my head?

Possible upcoming titles from the H-O-W series*

Backpacks: How to Know When They're Unhappy

Painting Things Green Without Telling Your Parents

Interstellar Satellite Construction and Repair

All Soda Is Made with the Livers of Pigs

Skateboarding: Sport of Fools

All Folders Should Be Blue and Here's Why

Cooking and Serving Bats and Ferrets to Large Groups

~~How to Build a Really Big Drum Set~~ CANCELLED! FORGET IT

Why Twisty Straws Threaten Peace

Water-Heater Repair and Construction

You Know How Everyone Was Talking About How Dolphins Were So Smart? Well, They Were Kidding. Dolphins Are Stupid. So, So Dumb.

Trains and Their Enemies, the Pennies of The North America

How to Harm People Who Play Drums

Carpets: What's Underneath? How to Find Out

Hippos? Hippos? Did You Say Hippos? I Thought That Was What You Said

246 Things They Won't Teach You in Karate School

Which Hands Taste Best
(NOT AVAILABLE TO SWEDES)

Basic Volcano Design

**subject to change*

ABOUT THE AUTHORS

Dr. Doris Haggis-On-Whey now has eighteen degrees from twenty institutions of higher learning and carpentry. She has traveled the world extensively, so much in fact that there are those who believe that Dr. H-O-W actually invented the world, in the late 1970s. This is not in fact true, but what is true is that she has written or will soon write over 156 definitive and Earth-changing books on such subjects as Whales, Big Whales, Advanced Electricity Usage, Puppetry, Cooking Food without Using Food, Matthew Perry, Orange Paper, Thrones, Orangeish-Yellow Paper, Post Office Design and Operation, Calculus for People from Small Towns, and Grease Theory and Construction.

Benny is the husband of Dr. Doris Haggis-On-Whey, and is hiding in the barn.

ABOUT THE DESIGNERS

Mark Wasserman and Irene Ng continue to have the privilege of working with Dr. Haggis-On-Whey. As they have chosen to not pursue a life of science, they are hardly worth discussing here. They still live in San Francisco.

Research assistance has been provided by the de la Manzana brothers, and by Dave and Toph Eggers.